A Closed Book

LA NOUVELLE AGENCE
7, rue Corneille
75006 PARIS

BLAKE FRIEDMANN
Literary, TV & Film Agency
122 Arlington Road
London NW1 7HP
Telephone: 0171 284 0408
FAX: 0171 284 0442
e-mail: 'firstname'@blakefriedmann.co.uk

A CLOSED BOOK

GILBERT ADAIR

faber and faber

First published in 1999
by Faber and Faber Limited
3 Queen Square London WC1N 3AU

Typeset by Faber and Faber Ltd
Printed in England by Clays Ltd, St Ives plc

© Gilbert Adair, 1999

Gilbert Adair is hereby identified as author of this
work in accordance with Section 77 of the Copyright,
Designs and Patents Act 1988

A CIP record for this book
is available from the British Library

ISBN 0–571–20081–8

2 4 6 8 10 9 7 5 3 1

for Thomas, Adrian and Urs

A story has been thought to its conclusion
when it has taken its worst possible turn.

FRIEDRICH DÜRRENMATT

A CLOSED BOOK

The blind is flapping at the window again. I don't care what anyone says, there really has to be a draught somewhere. I suppose I might get up and try to fix it. But, no, that's absurd, what on earth could I do? Besides, Ryder will be ringing the doorbell any minute now, or so I hope. He's late already. Slightly as yet, but late all the same. I can't abide unpunctuality. What was it someone said? That the trouble with punctuality is that there's never anyone there to appreciate it. Well, I would have been here to appreciate it! Though, to be fair, if he has motored down from London, it's possible – 'Aha, there he is now' – *the weekend traffic has been heavy.*

So, Mr Ryder. There you are and here I am. We shall see what we shall see.

'Who is it?'

'It's John Ryder? You were expecting me at three?'

'Yes, I was. Hold on. Let me just undo this damned chain.'

'No problem.'

'Come on, you! There! Yes, come in, will you.'

'Ah. Oh, well, thank you. I'm – I'm afraid I'm a few minutes late for our appointment, but I –'

'What? Not at all. Virtually on the dot. Which is a real achievement, in view of how isolated the house is. Did you have any problem locating it?'

'Not really. I followed to the letter the directions you gave me and I –'

'Good. Now. Please leave your coat, your things, whatever, on one of the chairs over by that wall. It's simpler than hanging them up.'

'Oh. Righto.'

'Good.'

'Do take the leather armchair. It's far the most comfortable.'

'Thanks.'

'I'll sit here, shall I? But maybe you'd care for a drink? I'm afraid whisky is all I have, but connoisseurs assure me it's good stuff.'

'I won't, thanks anyway. It's a little early for me.'

'Sorry I can't offer you any coffee. My housekeeper isn't around today, and without her it becomes a devilishly complicated business.'

'No, nothing at all, thanks. I'm absolutely fine. I had lunch of a sort on the motorway.'

'Of a sort? Yes, I do sympathize. Not at a Little Chef, I trust?'

'Hah! No, I managed to do better than that. Even so, it was muck.'

'Barbaric, quite barbaric. Ah me, it was – well, you know, Ryder, I was about to say it was ever thus, but the melancholy truth, as perhaps you're too young to realize, is that it wasn't ever thus. You quite comfortable there?'

'Very much so.'

'Good, good. Please feel free to smoke if you'd like to. Here, why not have one of mine? There ought to be an ashtray somewhere.'

'Uh, no thanks. I won't all the same.'

'Oh, I'm sorry. Maybe I put you off by so nonchalantly pulling a cigarette from my dressing-gown pocket?'

'No, not at all.'

'Forgive me. It's an old habit of mine. And I can never quite make up my mind if it's the height of elegance or the height of vulgarity.'

'It wasn't that at all. I've given up.'

'Wise man. Then perhaps we might start?'

'Certainly.'

'Well now, let's see. Given that our telephone conversation was rather laconic, I'm curious to know why you agreed to drive down for the interview.'

'Well?'

'Well, I suppose I –'

'Did it have something to do with the name?'

'The name? I'm afraid I don't follow?'

'My name. You must have noticed how similar to your own it is?'

'Yes, I did. Though I can't honestly claim that that influenced me.'

'Was it who I was, then? Had you heard of me?'

'Well, naturally I had. I'm a great admirer of yours.'

'Look, Ryder, perhaps you'd better tell me something about yourself. How old are you?'

'I'm thirty-three.'

'Thirty-three. And what about your recent past? Your line of work? On the telephone you said something about stocks and shares. Do you work in the City?'

'No, I play the market from home. I've made a packet too.'

'Have you now?'

'It's child's play as long as you're willing to devote all your time and energies to it.'

'So why would you want to exchange such child's play for a leap into the unknown?'

'Frankly, I'm bored.'

'Bored?'

'I'm beginning to feel like one of those loony old crones in Monte Carlo, you know, who stay at the roulette tables till they win exactly what they set out to win then immediately down tools and go home. I sit at the computer, I never see anyone, I never go out. Or if I do go out, I feel guilty and I wonder if something sensational's come up in my absence.'

'And has it?'

'Never. Which is why I feel I've got to do something, something challenging, something stimulating, with my life. Before it's too late.'

'Obviously you've no idea what this job of mine entails?'

'None at all.'

'And that doesn't worry you?'

'Look. All I've committed myself to so far is answering an advertisement in a newspaper and driving down the M40. If what you offer me – assuming you do have something to offer me – if it turns out to be, well, not of interest, then I'll just get back into the car and drive home the way I came.'

'Hmm. I'm pleased you're so candid. I like that. I also like the fact that you're opening up a little. I can imagine how intimidating this situation must be for you.'

'It is a bit.'

'Anyway, now is the time for me to catch that candour on the wing and ask the first really important – I mean the first really *relevant* – question of this interview.'

'Fire away.'

'How good are your powers of observation?'

'Sorry, my what?'

'How good are you at observing things? And describing what you've observed?'

'I'm afraid I don't understand.'

'Come, come. What you don't understand isn't the question but why I'm putting it to you, am I right? I have my reasons, I assure you, but never mind those for now. Just try to answer it. And no false modesty, please.'

'Well, like just about everyone, I suppose, I've got a pretty high opinion of my powers of observation. But who knows? I don't remember ever having them put to the test.'

'Then let's put them to the test right now, shall we? Why don't you describe this room for me and what's in it?'

'If you like. It's a large room, very dark, square – squar*ish* – with an ornate black marble fireplace – and on either side of the fireplace there are two leather chairs – they're also black – I'm sitting in one of them, you're sitting in the other. There are three smaller chairs lined up against the wall opposite us. They're red and, I'd say, eighteenth-century-looking. On the right of the fireplace there's a bust of what looks like a young mulatto woman. Would it be terracotta?'

'It's by Carpeaux. And, yes, it's terracotta. Go on.'

'On the mantelpiece there are six blue-and-white vases. Or maybe they're pots? Some of them have lids but, let me see, two, yes, two of them don't. They're all different shapes and sizes. The walls are interesting – very, very dark burnt ochre, the colour of dry, dusty old frescoes. They really look as though they – well, as though they could do with a good wash. Though that's probably the intended effect. In fact, I'm sure it's the intended effect. But if you don't mind me saying so, and you did ask me to be honest –'

'I did indeed.'

'Well, everything in the room is really dusty and discoloured.'

'Ah. Go on.'

'Behind you there's a floor-to-ceiling set of book-shelves. There's a card table and a gold music stand next to a large bay window and in the corner there's – what do you call it? – an escritoire? – with what look like handwritten documents and funny old scrolls poking out of the drawers. And a pear? Yes, it *is* a pear. Made of something like marble? – or jade? – I don't know. I should say it's been used as a paperweight.

Actually, it's all a bit like the den of some mediaeval scholar or saint.'

'Good, very very good. Go on.'

'Between the two of us there's a low wooden table. I'd call it a coffee table except that that wouldn't really convey the feel of it. It's like something from an old pub, an old cider pub, it's pretty chipped and scarred. There's a big pile of books on it. Actually, now I see them, they *are* coffee-table books. But the only one I can make out is the one on top and, at the angle I'm looking at it, it's upside down. It's called – it's called – *The Romantic Agony* and it's by – by Mario – Mario Praz.'

'The name is pronounced "Praz" and there were too many "theres" – "*there's* a card table", "*there's* a pile of books" – but otherwise that was excellent. It was so precise I felt almost as though I were there, ha ha! I shall need that precision.'

'Well, thank you.'

'Now let's try something a little trickier. Can you describe your face to me?'

'My face?'

'Yes, yes, your face. Describe to me exactly what you look like. What *it* looks like. Would you call yourself good-looking, for example?'

'Yes. Yes, if I'm honest, I'd have to say I *am* good-looking.'

'And?'

'Well, I'm what people tend to call, uh, willowy? Anyway, that's the word that's been used. You see, I'm slim, and thin-faced, with high cheek bones, prominent cheek bones, I suppose you'd call them. You know, this is all a bit embarrassing.'

'Just go on.'

'My nose is bony – but perfectly straight – and I've got, oh well, sort of liquid eyes. Sky-blue. I'm losing my hair. Though gradually, you know, I'm not there yet, just a receding hairline. It's dark, curly hair, what you'd call fluffy. Oh, and I've got a tiny mole at the corner of my left nostril.'

'Clean-shaven? Bespectacled?'

'Yes. And no. Look, would you mind telling me what –'

'Bear with me, man, I've nearly done. I want you now to describe *my* face.'

'Come now, don't tell me there's nothing to be said about it. I know better than that.'

'Let me tell you at once, John Ryder, you're of absolutely no use to me unless you describe my face.'

'If you wish. Your face has been – I would guess – badly damaged in an accident. The entire left side looks as though someone has been trying to pull it off.

Everything seems to slant downward, your mouth in particular. Which means that when you speak your lips seem to be chewing the words. And your skin – I'm still talking about the left side – your skin, I have to say, is a weird colour – kind of greeny-grey – is verdigris the word? – and there are scars, criss-crossing scars, and strange bulges on your temples. Like bubbles, almost. The right side seems pretty much untouched. It's hard to tell, but I'd say you were in your early sixties. You've got grey hair, lots of it, some would say too much. It's badly cut, it's too long at the neck. As for your eyes, well, I can't describe them, because you're wearing dark glasses.'

'Of course I am. How thoughtless of me. I'll take them off.'

'Well, John Ryder? Cat got your tongue?'

'You have no eyes.'

'That's quite right. I have no eyes. I'm not only blind, I'm not only sightless, I'm eyeless. And I don't wear glass eyes because I think having *two* glass eyes would be over-egging the rather soggy, lumpy pudding of my face, don't you agree?'

'Oh well. Congratulations anyway. To be frank, you might have been a trifle less zestful in your description, but I rather goaded you, didn't I?'

'I'm sorry if I –'

'No, no, no. You acquitted yourself admirably. You did just what I asked you to do.'

'Well, thank you. I must say, for a man with – for a man with no eyes, you certainly seem to know your way about.'

'This room, you mean? Oh, I've memorized this room. I've learned it off by heart, like a poem by Walter de la Mare. Still, there can be no hiding the fact that I'm blind. There's something, you see, about a blind man's movements. Have you ever heard of Herbert Marshall?'

'Herbert Marshall? No, I'm afraid not.'

'No, he would have been long, long before your time. A film star.'

'A blind film star?'

'Heavens no, he wasn't blind. But he *did* have an artificial leg. I fancy he lost the real one in the war. That would be the First World War. In any event, Herbert Marshall was one-legged, yet he never played a one-legged character on the screen. Not once. But what he did play, quite often, was blind men. Interesting, wouldn't you say? Yet it makes a sort of sense after all, because if you watch a blind man you'll see that he moves exactly as though he had a gammy leg.'

'Well, that's all by the by. However, just so as you

know – and if things work out as I hope, you will have to know – I lost my eyes, *and* the left half of my face, in Sri Lanka. My car skidded in the rain and flew clean off the highway. Or what passes for a highway in Sri Lanka. I was in what I think is called the suicide seat, next to the chauffeur, and my head went through the windscreen. Then the car burst into flames. And here you have the ghastly result. That was four years ago.'

'I'm sorry.'

'Thank you, but I'm afraid such commiseration has long since passed its sell-by date. As have all conventional expressions of sympathy. I wanted you to know, though, because I begin to think you might be the man for me. Whether you yourself will want the job is altogether another matter.'

'As I said, I'm intrigued.'

'Then let me tell you what it's all about. What I shall want from you are your eyes.'

'You what?'

'There's no need for alarm. I wish merely to borrow your eyes, not remove them. What I'm looking for, John Ryder, is an amanuensis. Someone whose eyes will take the place of mine. Someone capable not only of observing the world *for* me but of communicating his observations *to* me so that I can then transmute them into prose. Into *my* prose.'

'I think I understand. You plan to write a book?'

'Four years ago this terrible thing happened to me. I spent seven months in a Sri Lankan hospital and, during those seven months, during those seven endless months, I did, as they say, a lot of thinking. Thinking was all I could do, I was so swathed in bandages I must have resembled the Michelin Man. For I have to tell you, what you see, and horrible enough as it is for you, what you see is but the tip of the iceberg, to use a somewhat inappropriate metaphor. I suffered third-degree burns over most of my body.'

'Ah.'

'Now. You mentioned earlier that you admired me, am I right?'

'Yes, that's quite true.'

'What have you read?'

'Pretty much everything, I think. *Sitting at the Feet of Ghosts*, of course.'

'Of course. Typical. My weakest book, yet it's the one everyone's read. This country's as thick as two planks. You started with that one, did you? Or probably not even with the book itself but the film version?'

'Well, yes, I can't tell a lie. I'm afraid that *is* how it happened. I did see the film first and I liked it and then I read the novel.'

'Peuh!'

'But I did go on to read *The First Fruits, The Lion of Beltraffio, The Spirit of the Place*.'

'I believe you, I believe you!'

'Ah, I'm sorry, John. May I call you John? I'm sorry, that was rude of me. I really do believe you. Let me ask you something, though. Didn't you, a self-confessed admirer of my books, one of my faithful readers, didn't you ever wonder what had become of me?'

'I'm sorry?'

'Look, John, it's perfectly true I was never the most gregarious, never what you'd call the most clubbable, of authors. Even so, I was visible enough, I was seen around. I won prizes – the Booker, of course, for *Sitting at the Feet* – at one time there was even vague talk of the Nobel. Not that I lent credence to *that*. Still, I wasn't a recluse, I was invited to literary dos, I was happy to give interviews if asked nicely. Well, didn't you ever think, during the past four years, I wonder what on earth's become of old so-and-so?'

'I'm not sure I know how to answer that question. Sure, I read a lot, but I'm not what you'd call a literary type. I mean, I've never consciously followed a writer's career, even a writer I like. If I gave any thought to it at all, I suppose I must have assumed you were at work on some great slab of a novel which was taking you longer than usual. But, actually, I didn't give it any thought. I'm just rationalizing things after the event. It wasn't anything that specially preoccupied me.'

'Well, I suppose I'm pleased to hear that. I suppose. It's true, even when you're as famous as I was, if you drop out of circulation, people forget you ever existed. It's hard. Then again, I can't deny it's the way I wanted it to be, so I really don't have any grounds for complaint.'

'It *is* hard, though.'

'Anyway, *à nos oignons*, as the witty French say. Where was I? In a Sri Lankan hospital, I think. Well, the one good thing about losing both your eyes is of course that you never have to see what you look like without them. It's a bit like that old crack about the Eiffel Tower. When it was erected, someone, one of the Goncourt brothers, I suspect, remarked that he enjoyed looking out over Paris from the top of the Eiffel Tower because it was the one vantage point in the city from which he was spared the sight of the bloody thing itself. I, thank God, was spared the sight of my own sightlessness. Except that I still had my fingers, I hadn't lost them, and I could feel those criss-crossing scars and those "bubbles", as you so vividly described them, and those two matching holes in my face, those two empty sockets. And I made a resolution after my accident that I wouldn't inflict my face on anyone else ever again. For a while I even thought of staying on in

Sri Lanka. Like a leper. But that, you know, turned out to be far more complicated than returning home. A matter of credit cards, bank accounts, direct debits, all that sort of trivia.'

'I can imagine.'

'So what I did instead was creep back into Britain about a year later. I travelled the long way round, by boat, and I arrived in the dead of winter. I made certain of arriving in winter, so that I wouldn't look too incongruous all wrapped up and swathed about as I was. I came down here to the Cotswolds – I bought this house several years ago as a weekend retreat – I chose it specifically because it was so isolated, though I didn't know then just how handy that isolation would turn out to be – I came down here, as I say, and I went to ground. No newspapers. No wireless. No television. Nothing. The world could go hang for all I cared.'

'You never go out?'

'Would *you* go out? How would *you* like to hear children screaming as you walk by? No, I tell a lie. Children don't scream. They're hardier little creatures than that. They tug at their mothers' coat-tails and they shout, "Mummy, Mummy, look at the funny man! Look at the man with no face!" And their mortified mothers try to shush them up. Try *most* of the time. All that, I have heard.'

'Did you ever consider plastic surgery?'

'Did I ever consider plastic surgery? My dear John, what you're looking at is the product of plastic surgery. All of this – this, this and this – even this, look at it, give it a tug, go on, do – all of this is *after*, not *before*. My face may resemble a jigsaw puzzle now, but at least only two of the pieces are actually missing.'

'And you say you've remained here, indoors, ever since?'

'No. No, it's true, I used to go out. In the evening. In those days, though, I had a friend. Charles. He was an Oxford don. I ought to say, a former Oxford don. He lived in Chipping Campden. That, as you may or may not know, is a small town about thirty miles from here.'

'I do know Chipping Campden.'

'Well, my friend Charles lived in Chipping Campden and once, occasionally twice, a week, he'd drive over and dine with me. Then, after dark, he'd take me out for a stroll. Always after dark. It's for that reason I always long for summer to come to an end.'

'Sorry, for what reason?'

'In winter, you see, it's dark by – when? – by four o'clock? In summer we had to wait until at least nine or ten and even then there was a fairly good chance of meeting someone else out walking. And I couldn't cover my face up quite so plausibly, of course, on a balmy summer evening. I tell you, John, some of the

worst moments of my existence have been hot summer nights when I've been out for a stroll. People may
not say anything, but I can hear them. I can hear the
way their conversation falters and then falls eerily
quiet and then starts up again when they imagine
they're out of earshot, but they're not, you see. It's
always just that crucial little bit too soon. Do you
know, I've actually heard cars slowing down – *slowing
down* – presumably so their gawping occupants can
get a better look at me. And dogs. There are dogs that
actually bark at me.'

'You know, you probably won't believe me, but it
isn't honestly that bad. I can't help feeling you're over –'

'I know how bad it is.'

'Didn't you ever think of having a dog yourself? You
know, one of those – what are they called? – seeing-eye
dogs? They're Labradors usually.'

'Can't abide the nasty slavering beasts. Never
could. I detest barking. To me a barking dog sounds
just like some asthmatic old buffer coughing up his
guts. *And* dogs work for the police.'

'They what?'

'You've never heard of a police cat, have you?'

'Hah. Well no, I guess not.'

'I'm basically a cat person. I had one once, a
Siamese. No longer, though. My face would give even
a cat the willies. But to return to Charles. Poor fellow

died on me last year. And now I have no one. No one but an illiterate housekeeper who cooks for me and keeps the place reasonably neat. Or so I thought. Till you let slip how grubby it was.'

'Now look, sorry, but there you're being a bit unfair, both to me and your housekeeper. I didn't say the house, the room, was dirty. Just that it clearly hasn't been painted in some years. Anyway, I like it the way it is.'

'Enough to come and stay and help me write my book?'

'Well, I don't really know. What exactly *would* that entail?'

'You'd have to live here, of course. Seven days a week, if you're so minded. Five, if you preferred to return to London for two days out of every seven. And, by the way, those two days wouldn't have to be Saturday and Sunday. As I'm sure you must realize, weekends have no meaning for me.'

'I meant the nature of the work itself. You said earlier you wanted to "borrow" my eyes?'

'Yes. What I intend to write is – for want of a better word, I suppose I'll have to call it my autobiography. In any event, whatever it precisely is, it'll be my last book. My testament, if you like. And what I need from you, or whoever, is actually, physically, to write the bloody thing for me. Now I know I must strike you as a cantankerous old bugger. That was certainly my reputation in what is laughingly referred to as London's literary world. But I'm not such a fogey as all that. In my study, for example – that's the door to it on your right – I have what I think is called a state-of-the-art word processor. I purchased it only a couple of weeks before I flew to Sri Lanka.'

'Really? Now I'd have put you down as a pen-and-ink sort of writer.'

'Well, as it happens, old man, not quite, not quite. I've actually been known to use a typewriter, believe it or not. But it's quite true, I always had the impression that with a computer writing precedes thinking rather than the other way about.'

'So why did you buy one?'

'You might say I got it on prescription. I was having problems with posture. Or overusing one of my finger muscles, I don't recall. The upshot, anyway, was that my doctor prescribed a word processor. Unfortunately, I still hadn't got the hang of it when the calamity struck.'

'I'm afraid to have to tell you, but it's no longer state-of-the-art.'

'What?'

'It must be quite a crock by now.'

'Why, that's nonsense. It's only four years old.'

'*Only* four years? You don't seem to realize, but computer technology advances so quickly a new model's out of date the day you buy it.'

'You don't say? What an extraordinary way to run a business.'

'I assure you.'

'Fair enough. You must know best. It only goes to show how time has stood still for me. But not to worry, I'll have the very latest machine bought for the job. What's more important than the writing, though, is the preparation.'

'The preparation?'

'Tell me, John, have you ever watched a child, by that I mean an infant, a baby, pointing its finger at something?'

'No, I can't say I particularly have.'

'Aha, you see. If you *were* to work with me, that's just the sort of observation I'd need from you. Anyway, the principal difference between an adult and a child pointing a finger is that the adult first notices something of interest to him then points at it so that others, his friends, his companions, whoever, can share in that interest. Right?'

'Right.'

'Well, with a child, the process is reversed. It points its finger at the outside world more or less indiscriminately. And then, *and only then*, does it look to see what it might happen to be pointing at. And since for a child the whole world constitutes a source of discovery, it's invariably and inevitably something interesting that it finds in its field of vision. Interesting to the child, at least.'

'I'm sure you're right, though I can't say I've ever noticed it.'

'I take it, then, you have no children of your own?'

'Uh, no. I'm not married.'

'Good. That's to say, it's good in the sense that it's good for me. If you *do* decide to take the job.'

'But you still haven't explained.'

'Explained?'

'Pointing the finger?'

'I resemble that child, John. I cannot point my finger at anything specific. I can only point it indiscriminately and then send *you* – let's say you, for the sake of the argument – then send *you* off to see what it is I've pointed at. To see and then report back to me.'

'Yes, I get you. You'd be sending me off to places you've known at different periods of your life, is that it? Your childhood haunts, that sort of thing?'

'Yes, well, maybe. In fact, certainly.'

'But?'

'But?'

'It sounded as though you were about to add something?'

'It's true, I was. You must understand, John, I have no interest in writing a conventional autobiography. You're familiar with the kind of thing, I'm sure. "I was born blah blah blah." "I went to school blah blah blah." "When I went up to Oxford, little did my tutor realize blah blah blah." Ideally, I see this book as a summation, a *summa summarum*, of all my thoughts, my ideas, my thematic preoccupations. The autobiography, if you like, of my soul, of my inner life. Or at least as much as my outer life. I loathe those autobiographies that offer the reader nothing more than what you might call the minutes of a life. Minutes, you know? Like the minutes taken down at a board meeting?'

'Yes, I got that.'

'Ah, forgive me, John. I'm so used to not being got.'

'That's all right. May I ask, though, do you have a title for it?'

'A tentative title. *Truth and Consequences*.'

'Oh yes, I like that. Very, very much.'

'Do you? I myself am not entirely convinced.'

'Oh, why?'

'Strikes me it's a trifle pretentious.'

'No, I wouldn't say so. No, not at all. In my opinion, for what it's worth, you should keep it.'

'For a while I toyed with *The Death of the Reader* – I trust you get the pun? – but I liked that even less. Well, we'll see. So what about it, John? Does the chance of working with me on this new book appeal to you?'

'Well, I –'

'I won't pretend I'm an easy man to get along with. But doubtless you've already gathered that?'

'Well? Is it yes or no? Or maybe you'd like time to think it over?'

'Uh, we haven't actually spoken about –'

'Yes?'

'Well, about money.'

'You mean remuneration? You're quite right, we haven't. Well, John, I'll tell you, I'm a rich man. Not, as they say nowadays, seriously rich but quite rich enough not to have to worry about mundane money matters. We'll discuss the question in detail once you've actually said yes, but off the top of my head – what's left of my head, that is – I'd be prepared – yes, I'd be prepared to pay you, say, three thousand a month. If that seems reasonable?'

'That seems extremely generous.'

'Then let's say three thousand pounds a month. Plus of course board and lodging for as long as it's necessary. A year ought to do it, if we buckle down to the job. Plus, naturally, a modest percentage of all moneys accruing to me from the book itself. I mean, royalties, translation rights, subsidiary rights, serialization rights, book club sales and all the rest of it. Normally, I do rather well by my writing.'

'Then – yes. Yes.'

'Good. I'm very pleased, John. And now you must call me Paul. You eventually will, so why keep up the formalities in the meantime?'

'Very well – Paul.'

'There's one more thing. Minor, but I want you to know exactly what you're getting into.'

'Yes?'

'I don't expect you, and indeed I wouldn't want you, to be nursemaid to me. As I say, my housekeeper – she's a Mrs Kilbride, by the way. Glaswegian, poor dear. Well, Mrs Kilbride cleans and cooks for me, and I make various arrangements about meals when she has her days off. So you needn't worry about that.'

'Actually, I enjoy cooking. And I'm not bad. I'd be glad to make the odd supper for the two of us if you'll let me. Frankly, living alone, I don't often get the chance.'

'Well. Well, I must say that would be a delightful bonus. Poor Mrs Kilbride does her very best, I imagine, but I'm afraid her repertoire is woefully limited. But only when you fancy it, you understand. I shall be working you quite hard during the day.'

'Cooking isn't work for me.'

'So much the better. Anyway, what I started to say

was that there are one or two chores, domestic chores, which I'll have to call on you for. Fear not. Nothing too demanding.'

'I can't see that that would be a problem.'

'For example, I still enjoy my walks in the evening, and since Charles's death these have had to be frustratingly curtailed – to the point where I'm beginning to feel I'm under house arrest. I hope you wouldn't mind taking his place?'

'Absolutely not. I'm sure I'll feel like a walk myself.'

'There's nothing to it. To walking a blind man, I mean. You just gently take my arm and let me know when we reach the edge of the pavement, or when there are steps to go up or down, anything that might trip me up.'

'Uh huh.'

'The other chore . . . Now this is slightly humiliating.'

'I have a fear of the dark, John. I have a terrific fear of the dark.'

'A fear of the dark?'

'I know, I know. It makes no sense for a blind man to be afraid of the dark. But there you are and there it is. I've always been claustrophobic. *I feel claustrophobic in the universe.*'

'Wow. That *is* claustrophobic.'

'It's no laughing matter.'

'Sorry, I didn't mean –'

'Even on a, shall I say, on a non-existential level, my claustrophobia has posed all sorts of problems for me. I was never able to take the Tube, for example, and lifts – well, lifts were always a nightmare. Because sometimes you just have to take them, don't you? In New York, for example. But, you know, even in New York, I recall once having to walk up twelve flights of stairs in some friend's apartment block because the lift – the elevator – looked to me just like a coffin that someone had stood upright. I'd always have to insist on being given the lower floors in hotels, I'd always keep the curtains slightly ajar when I was sleeping in a strange bed so there wouldn't be any risk of my waking up in the night in total darkness.'

'And nothing has changed since you lost your sight?'

'If anything, it's worse. The point is, John, I'll expect you to behave in this house just as though I *could* see. This is *most* important. The lights should be switched on at exactly the same time as they would be in a normal household. Even if I should be sitting in here by myself, the light *has* to be on. I simply couldn't bear the thought of sitting alone in the dark. I always put the light on in the evening when I come into a room and you must too, you understand?'

'Yes, of course.'

'Most particularly the bathroom light.'

'The bathroom?'

'Yes, the bathroom. I shall have to ask you – it's another little chore I must mention – but I'll have to ask you to keep an eye on the bathroom light for me. I hope you won't mind?'

'Not at all, but –'

'The thing is, I have this habit. I sing in the bath. I really do. And I'm going to surprise you here, if I'm not mistaken, because what I sing are popular songs. Not pop songs, you understand, God forbid, but, well, songs from a bygone era, Jerome Kern, Cole Porter, Rodgers and Hammerstein, that sort of thing. I have a vast collection of these songs inside my head. Here, intact, in my memory. And I really couldn't endure the idea of soaping myself in a bathtub while chortling "You're the Top" or "Cheek to Cheek" or "Alexander's Ragtime Band" – *in the dark*. In pitch darkness, you understand. I just couldn't endure it.'

'I'll see the light is on.'

'And the door ajar? You'll see that the door is always ajar?'

'Yes, that too.'

'You may feel a little squeamish at first about the bathroom door being ajar, but it's got to be, I'm afraid. There *is* a window in the bathroom, but it's narrow and very high, anyway quite impossible for me to reach, and if the door were closed, well, it's not that there'd be any problem really, the doorknob is a perfectly average type of doorknob. Still, I'd have a moment or two of panic while I groped for it and I know those moments of panic and I'd prefer not to go through that again. It's pathetic, I know, but it's the way I am. So you'll make sure the door is left ajar, won't you?'

'I promise you. You'll never be left alone in the dark.'

'Good, good. Then let's change the subject, shall we? It's time we talked of practicalities. When would you be able to start?'

'I suppose almost at once.'

'Monday?'

'Monday? Let's see. Today is Saturday. Yes. Yes, I don't see why not. No, wait. Could we say Tuesday? Or even Wednesday? Wednesday?'

'Certainly, if you –'

'It's the weekend, you see. I'll need to put some affairs in order first. And I can only do that on a weekday.'

'Wednesday would be perfectly acceptable.'

'In fact, if I drove back to London this afternoon and, yeah, I could pack tomorrow, wind up my various affairs on Monday, maybe Tuesday as well, then drive down here again on Tuesday evening. How does that sound?'

'That sounds fine, John. The delay may actually be a blessing in disguise. It'll give me time to arrange for the new computer to be ordered. And, maybe, with your expertise in these matters, you might point me in the right direction? I confess I haven't the foggiest notion where to start.'

'If you prefer – Paul – why don't you leave all that to me? With an extra twenty-four hours in London, I could buy a new computer and bring it with me in the car, say, on Wednesday evening. We could settle up later.'

'Now that *is* a kind suggestion. Not later than Wednesday, though, if you don't mind. I'm extremely eager to get started. The more so now I've found my collaborator.'

'Wednesday it'll be. I promise.'

'Wonderful. Well, John, maybe you'd like that drink now? We might raise a toast to our collaboration.'

'Yes, let's.'

'If you'd be mother.'

'Sure.'

'The drinks are on the cabinet behind you. I repeat, there's nothing but whisky. But it's good whisky.'

'Whisky's fine. How do you take yours?'

'Neat, please. And don't ask me to say when.'

'I must say, Paul, I do admire your capacity to – to laugh at yourself. Well, not to laugh at yourself, exactly. But to be able to joke about your predicament. You obviously haven't lost your sense of humour.'

'*Lost* my sense of humour? That's a laugh in itself. It was only when I lost my sight that I actually acquired a sense of humour.'

'I don't follow.'

'I soon learned, my friend, that a blind man has to be the salt of the earth. He has to be, you understand? I *abominate* being the salt of the earth. As you can imagine, it's certainly never come naturally to me. But that's what I have to be if I mean to survive. People, you see, people may be initially intrigued by blindness, they're curious, they're even rather fascinated, but they soon weary of its charms. It's creepy. It's macabre. Worst of all, it's atrociously time-consuming. "Please do this for me." "Please fetch that for me." "Would you be so kind as to open this door or close that door?" The blind are a frightful burden on those with eyes, and there inevitably comes a moment when we're made to feel, and with a vengeance, just what a burden we are. By the way, I hope what I'm saying isn't giving you second thoughts?'

'Don't worry about me.'

'What the blind discover is that they must never, *never*, whinge. "Whinge" – there's the new word one starts to hear. To hear and fear. "Excuse me, but I've lost my sight." "Oh, don't whinge!" "But, you don't understand, I have no eyes." "Oh, stop whingeing, for Christ's sake!"'

'Come now, don't tell me people actually say that to your – to –'

'To my face, John? If you mean to my face, then say so. It may not be a pretty picture, but I still *have* a face of sorts. And the answer to the question is, no. Not literally. But unless you learn to treat, to *wear*, your blindness lightly –'

'Here you are.'

'Sorry?'

'Your whisky.'

'Ah. Thank you. But, if I may, John. You must always take my hand first, then place the glass in it. Otherwise, you see, I've no way of knowing where it is.'

'Of course. Sorry.'

'You'll learn. As I was saying, though, unless you shrug off your affliction as though it were no more than some mildly inconvenient impediment, the standard of physical and moral support you receive from others goes into dramatically precipitous decline. A sense of humour is as indispensable to a blind man as a white stick.'

'I see.'

'But that's enough of gloom and doom. What I want you to appreciate, John, is that I really am pleased we're going to be working together, I really am. So. So here's to *Truth and Consequences*.'

'To *Truth and Consequences*.'

'Chin chin.'

'Chin chin.'

∾

The die is cast. So how do I feel? Uneasy, uneasy. Weren't I blind, I wouldn't countenance having a complete stranger living in my house. I never did care for guests 'sleeping over'. Not even Charles if I could help it. Not my style. But then, blindness has altered so much, my style along with everything else. In any event, I detect more than a hint of deference in his voice that must be a good sign. Somewhat colourless, at least so far, but that's all right and he'll probablythaw as we get to know each other. Inevitable if he's to live here, so deference isn't a bad point of departure. Not too stupid, either, which is convenient. No, allinall, I think I've made a good and suitable choice. God knows, I might have done worse.

∾

'Ah, John. So you've been unpacking, have you?'

'Yes, thanks. It's a very nice room. I feel sure I'm going to be comfortable in it.'

'Well, I hope so. And if there's anything you need, just ask.'

'Right. Uh, shall I sit here? Opposite you?'

'As far as I recall, there *is* no other seating place. You managed to settle all your affairs in London?'

'Uh huh. And tomorrow I'll install the computer. It's a Mac. It's what I use. I hope that's all right?'

'I told you before I know nothing of these machines. Whatever you feel at ease with.'

'It's just that there are, well, two schools of thought about current computers, Macs and PCs. The PCs are winning the battle – I should say, they've already won it – but I'm one of a dwindling band of Mac loyalists.'

'If a Big Mac is what you're used to, then that's the one you've got to have. I wonder what's keeping poor Mrs Kilbride.'

'When I came downstairs, I heard her pottering about in the kitchen.'

'Yes, well, she knows I like to be served at seven-thirty on the dot. What time is it now?'

'Nearly twenty-to.'

'Tsk. I dare say she's being extra-conscientious because of you. Oh, and John, she serves the plates straight on to the table. Simpler that way. Do you mind?'

'Course not.'

'And here, unless my ears deceive me, which would be *all* I need, here she is now. Mrs Kilbride, good Mrs Kilbride, John and I were starting to wonder what had become of you.'

'Well, sir, an Mister Ryder, ah'm sorry, ah'm so used to doin fur one ah had to rethink ma whole way of thinkin, seein there's two a you.'

'And what culinary *bonne bouche* have you whipped up for us tonight?'

'Careful ye dinnay touch the plate, it's hot. Bein as it's a kind a special evenin, ah made yer favourite. Steak and kidney pud.'

'But, Mrs Kilbride, as you well know, everything you cook is my favourite.'

'Here ye are, Mister Ryder. An dinnay ye worry. Ah know Sir Paul's pullin ma leg. Ah know how he talks about ma cookin behind ma back. But he knows he's got to like it or lump it.'

'Sir Paul's said nothing.'

'Oh yes he has. We go a long way back together, him an me. Don't we, you?'

'Yes, yes. If you must put it that way. And please don't dig your elbow into my ribs. You know I don't like it. Have we both been served?'

'It's all on the table.'

'Good. Well, John'll call you when we're done.'

'Dinnay ye let him bully ye, Mister Ryder. Else he'll become unbearable.'

'Shhhst, woman! Off with you!'

'John, there ought to be a bottle of wine somewhere.

And a corkscrew. If the old biddy hasn't forgotten them.'

'They're there! They're right there!'

'I thought you'd gone.'

'Ah'm goin'!'

'Good!'

'Now, John, if you wouldn't mind opening the bottle.'

'Of course.'

'She *has* gone now, I take it?'

'Yes.'

'You know, I've never seen her.'

'Mrs Kilbride?'

'She only started doing for me on my return from Sri Lanka, you know. Perhaps you'd care to describe her for me?'

'But surely your friend Charles must have done that?'

'Well, naturally he did, though it was some years ago now. The thing is, John, tomorrow we start work, tomorrow I mean to start borrowing your eyes, and it would be useful if you got some practice in this evening. Just casually, you know. Take your time.'

'Well – by the way, Paul, your glass is filled – well, let me see, she's in her late fifties, quite well preserved, actually surprisingly slim. I say surprisingly, because anyone just hearing her voice would definitely suppose she was fat. Well, not exactly fat. But she does have a sort of "plump" voice, sort of motherly.'

'Please, please, John. Don't you think it rather perverse of you under the circumstances to be describing her voice, the one thing about the woman with which I'm thoroughly familiar?'

'I just meant that, physically, she's not like her voice at all. Anyway, her hair, I suspect, is dyed, but very discreetly, no blue rinse rubbish or anything of that kind. And, really, I don't know what more I can say.'

'Think, man, think. You can't be racking your brains already?'

'Well. Well, I don't know whether you're aware of this, *or* whether I should be telling you, but she winks a lot.'

'She winks? What on earth do you mean?'

'Please don't let her know I said this. But when she was talking about the meal, and you were pretending to think everything she cooked was wonderful, she'd be winking at me as though to –'

'Ah yes, I see what you mean. Yes, I've been told that before. Yes, I can live with that. In the tragedy of my life she's bravely chosen to cast herself in the role of comic relief. One of my fool doctors must have advised her to be relentlessly chipper at all times, even to crack the odd joke about my blindness. So I don't subside into maudlin self-pity, I suppose. What was she wearing?'

'What was she wearing? Let's see. She had on a plastic apron with a recipe for Welsh rarebit stencilled on it – I think it was an advertisement for Lea & Perrins sauce – and, underneath that, a light pink jumper, angora or mohair, I can't be sure. Her skirt I couldn't see at all because of the apron. And, as I told you already, she's not nearly as big-bosomed as you'd think from just listening to her. Or is that reprehensibly sexist of me?'

'Well, I don't know about sexist, but it's certainly not an appetizing picture to conjure up just as I'm about to start eating. Which reminds me of another little domestic chore I forgot to mention. There won't be too many more of these, I promise you.'

'I told you, Paul, it's not a problem.'

'Well, if we're going to be lunching and dining *tête-à-tête*, I've got to teach you the clock method.'

'The clock method?'

'Let me explain. I have in front of me, as have you, a plate of steak and kidney pudding accompanied by, if I may hazard a guess, roast potatoes and Brussels sprouts. Or possibly peas?'

'Sprouts.'

'Sprouts it is. Good old dependable Mrs Kilbride. So, John, I know *what* is on my plate but I don't know precisely *where* it is. Which is where the clock method comes in. What I'll have to ask you –'

'Wait. I think I've understood. See if I have. Uh, steak and kidney at three o'clock. Sprouts at six. No, half-past five. Potatoes at nine. Have I got it?'

'Well done. Except, we're not talking synchronized watches here, so no half-hours or quarter-hours. Just stick to the basics.'

'Right.'

'Now tuck in, as Mrs Kilbride would say in her plump and motherly voice.'

'Can I give you some salt or pepper?'

'Neither, thank you.'

'Bread?'

'No thanks.'

'Righto.'

'And no righto either. Sorry. It's just one of those breezy expressions I can't stand.'

'Sorry, I –'

'That may have sounded like rudeness, John, but it was really just frankness, the sort of frankness that's absolutely essential between collaborators. Best to iron out all the little wrinkles at once, don't you agree? In fact, when I think of it, maybe there's something I do that *you* already know you're going to dislike. If so, speak up. It'll be easier for both of us in the long run.'

'As a matter of fact, there is something.'

'There is? Really? Hah, well, that's one on me. Well, well, well.'

'Well, what is it?'

'Poor. The word "poor".'

'Poor? Now it's my turn not to follow.'

'A moment ago you referred to Mrs Kilbride as "poor" Mrs Kilbride.'

'So?'

'And the first time I came here I heard you call your friend Charles "poor" Charles.'

'Yes?'

'I'm not sure I can explain.'

'Try nevertheless.'

'Well, I've never been able to stomach that tic of calling everyone "poor". It just seems so patronizing.'

'You did ask.'

'No, no, no, you were quite right to speak up. It's just that I never – do I really do that?'

'Actually, if I'm honest, I don't know. After all, I only met you for the first time last, what? Saturday? Maybe you don't. I wouldn't have mentioned it if you hadn't invited me to be frank. I hope I haven't offended you.'

'No. No, I'm not at all offended. Just a trifle taken aback. I never knew I did that. It comes as something of a mild shock. If I had an eyebrow to raise, I'd be raising it now.'

'I'm really sorry, I shouldn't have spoken.'

'Nonsense. I invited you to and you did. I trust, though, I have no other little "hang-ups" you wish to bring to my attention?'

'No, none.'

'Did I say something funny, John?'

'What?'

'You're smiling. Why are you smiling?'

'Smiling? You can *hear* me smile?'

'Be warned, John Ryder. I can hear you think.'

'So tell me. Why *were* you smiling?'

'Only because of the gesture you made.'

'The gesture I made?'

'Holding your fingers in the air. Inverted commas. When you used the word "hang-ups". It seemed unlike you somehow.'

'The gesture or the word?'

'Both, I guess.'

'These days there's so much about me that's unlike me.'

'Mmm. I've refilled your glass, by the way.'

'What? Oh, thanks. Enjoying your steak and kidney pud?'

'Yes. It's quite tasty.'

'It is what it is. Will you be wanting coffee later?'

'Yes please.'

'Then I'd advise you to alert Mrs Kilbride now. She tends to take her time. Just give her a shout, will you?'

'Me?'

'Why not?'

'Well, I don't know. It's my very first evening here.'

'She's going to be doing for you now as well as for me, isn't she?'

'Well . . . if you think so. Mrs Kilbride!'

'Gracious, she'll certainly have no excuse for not hearing that.'

'Sorry if I startled you. I'm going to need a bit more time to judge these things properly.'

'You'll have plenty of time. Incidentally, we might take a walk together later, John. If you feel up to it. Let you see something of the countryside. What do you say?'

'I was going to suggest it myself.'

'Good. Then it's a date.'

❧

'Which is yours?'

'Second one to the left. The voluminous one.'

'You mean the fur coat?'

'I've had it a good many years now. I got it in Chicago, long before all that fucking political correctness crap. I tell you, John, if ever some militant were to come up and tick me off for wearing fur, I'd just bare my eyes at her, so to speak. That might help her get things into perspective. Thanks. Just point my arm into the sleeve, will you?'

'You saying you've actually been harangued by anti-fur protestors?'

'Alas, no. I've never been given the chance to do my bogey-man number. Scarf, please. It ought to be hanging on the same peg as the coat.'

'Oh. Right. Here you are.'

'Thank you.'

'No stick?'

'You're my stick. Are we ready?'

'I am.'

'Open the door, will you?'

'As I told you, John, there's absolutely nothing to shepherding a blind man around, especially in a spot as lonely as this. Just slip your arm in mine – no, like this – good – and let me know either by telling me or exerting pressure on my arm – in fact, both to start with – let me know whenever there's something ahead of me I ought to be aware of. When we step off the kerb, for example. Or on to it of course.'

'Pressure? Like this, you mean?'

'Yes, that's good, only not so hard. Just as though you were gently reining in a horse. Do you ride?'

'No, I don't.'

'Too bad. Well then, it's like leading on the dance floor. You do dance?'

'Sorry. No again.'

'Oh well, use your imagination. Yes, but please don't do it unless there really is something I've got to watch out for. It can be confusing.'

'No, no, I did it that time because there are three steps coming up. I mean, going down.'

'Yes, yes, those I *am* aware of. At this stage of the game I don't have to be told about the steps at the end of my own garden path.'

'Sorry. It's not as easy as it looks.'

'Yes, it is. And you're doing very well. And, incidentally, John, you mustn't be surprised to hear me use expressions like "seeing" and "watching out". To you it may seem a curious choice of words, but it's amazing how much of a blind man's time is spent having to think about watching out for things or looking out for things.'

'I understand. Only I didn't say anything, you know.'

'I heard you think it. Remember what I told you.'

'I also remember Mrs Kilbride telling me not to let you bully me.'

'You can look after yourself. Okay. Left or right? Right, I think. Down into the village itself.'

'Towards the church?'

'That's right. What kind of evening is it? It feels fresh. Starlit.'

'It is. It's a beautiful night. Just beyond the common there are some fields –'

'I know them.'

'I was going to say, directly above those fields there's a full moon encircled by a sort of misty yellow halo. Almost like a grubby yellow halo.'

'"A full moon encircled by a misty yellow halo." Why, John, you make it sound like the title of a Japanese film.'

'A Japanese film? Sorry, I don't get that. Not much of a film buff, I'm afraid.'

'Not to worry. It was just a leetle bit precious. Preciosity, if truth be told, has always been my *péché mignon*. Except . . . Actually, when I think of it, it's a description I might just be able to use. You never can tell. Next time we're out walking, bring a notebook with you so you can jot down anything that might serve for the book. Understand, I certainly don't regard every remark I make as a priceless gem to be held in trust for posterity. But, as I say, I never know where or when ideas are likely to come to me. And it would be foolish not to make sure they don't evaporate before I've had time to decide whether they can be made to serve or not.'

'So there *is* such a thing as inspiration? Careful.

We're stepping off the kerb to cross the road.'

'Thanks. I tell you, John, inspiration has been discredited as a critical concept. Rightly so. Yet every artist *knows* it exists. There are moments when you just can't *put down* what you write, and it's usually those passages that the reader won't be able to put down either. But, I repeat, my little conceit about the moon –'

'Up on the kerb.'

'It was nothing, nothing at all. Please don't delude yourself I'm taking it more seriously than it deserves to be taken.'

'I find it fascinating. Seeing how your ideas arrive.'

'It's not even a real idea. But, if you wouldn't mind, try to remember it when we get back. I'll give you a notebook to jot it down in. Now where are we? I haven't been paying attention.'

'We're walking towards the churchyard. There's a bowling green on our left with a big white clubhouse.'

'Ah yes, the village bowling green. If ever you chance to be here on a Sunday afternoon, you really must wander down and watch the ladies of the local team in their thick woollen stockings and sensible white shoes. The sound of big black smooth bowling balls clicking together is a tonic for frazzled nerve-ends. You should try it.'

'I might at that.'

'So. The church is directly ahead of us?'

'That's right.'

'Able to date it at all?'

'Romanesque?'

'Romanesque? I seriously doubt it. But I know nothing of architecture. The churchyard's normally closed at this hour, so let's take the main village road, shall we? And let's also have a running commentary.'

'Determined to keep me on my toes?'

'For me, John, there's more to it than simply putting you through your paces.'

'Kerb.'

'Thank you. In spite of everything, I want to live. Damn it, I still want to live! To live in the world, in the real world! And it's no sinecure, I can tell you, whatever people may say about blindness and deafness.'

'Blindness and deafness?'

'I remember – I remember, before my accident – I'd like to see someone dare to make the same claim to my face now – but I remember dinner-party conversations about the advantages – the disadvantages as well – the respective advantages and disadvantages of blindness and deafness. And, you know, the consensus was always that the deaf were the worst off of the two. *Worse* off, I should say. The same whiskery old arguments would be trotted out. The deaf were cut off from the world – no conversation, no music, no Mozart – for some reason, the only composer ever cited was Mozart – they were cut off to a degree that simply wasn't true of the blind. What rubbish! What fucking godawful tripe! The world, John, the world was meant, the world was *designed*, to be seen! To be *seen*! Everything else in it, everything, even Mozart, is secondary to what is there to be seen. I know that now.'

'I'm sure you're right.'

'Then you must understand how important it is that you describe that world to me and describe it accurately. There at least is one advantage we the blind have over the deaf. Just try describing a Mozart piano concerto to a deaf man.'

'Well . . . given that he'd be as deaf to the description as to the piano concerto . . .'

'You know what I mean.'

'It's just that you must be so familiar with this village I didn't see much point in –'

'No? Well, think of it. If I were out walking, and assuming I still had my eyes about me, I'd be looking around as I walked, now wouldn't I? No matter how familiar I was with the village? I'm an observant man, John, I always was. And I haven't become any less observant now that I can no longer see anything.'

'You're right. So. Okay. Well, we've passed the church and now we're on a street that seems to be taking us out of the village altogether. I didn't see any wall plaque, so I can't tell you its name.'

'Its name is Cumberland Row. But that doesn't matter. Go on.'

'At the moment we're walking alongside the church graveyard. It looks rather spooky in the moonlight, rather surrealistic, and there's a British Legion clubhouse and the only shop I've noticed so far. Seems to be a combined greengrocer's, tobacconist's and Post Office. There are lots of postcards pinned up in the window. Let me see. Newborn puppies for sale. Sealyham terriers, if you're interested. Second-hand Land Rover. Amateur dramatic society production of *Witness for the Prosecution*. Cleaning woman.'

'That could be our Mrs Kilbride. She's always on the lookout for new clients.'

'There's no name. Just a telephone number. I can't read it without –'

'Oh, never mind, never mind. If it's hers, I have it at home. If it isn't, who cares? Learn to be more selective, more lapidary. Try to give the material a proper shape and structure.'

'Now we're passing in front of a tearoom. Mrs Effingham's Tea Shop. Correctly spelt, no "Oldes" or "Shoppes". Next door to that is what looks like a shoe-repair store. There's a cobbler's last in the window and some pairs of women's shoes. Very dusty-looking. Been there a long time, I should say. Mostly sort of broguey. And that would seem to be the last of the commercial premises. No, no, I'm wrong. There's a lighted building ahead on this side of the street – kerb coming up – could be a pub or a hotel.'

'It's both. Any signs of life?'

'Yes, there are. There's a small group of people standing in front of it. They must just have had a drink there. Two couples – middle-aged – well, middle-aged going on elderly. Well-dressed. One of the women is drawing on a pair of gloves. They're leaning against two cars parked next to each other. Half on the street, half on the pavement. A Volvo and, I should say, a Bentley.'

'So we're approaching them now, are we?'

'Yeah.'

'Look, Paul, if you'd prefer, there's a pleasant little path – there's a narrow little pathway just ahead of us to the left that we can still turn off into. I'm thinking about what you told me the other day? The worst moments in your life?'

'Well. Well, no, what the hell. It's going to happen to us, it's going to happen to you, sooner or later, it might as well happen now, tonight. Besides, it might not happen at all. It doesn't always. Let them see my face. At least I won't have to look at their ugly mugs.'

'Okay. If that's the way you want it.'

'Well?'

'What?'

'Was there any reaction?'

'No punches pulled, please. I can take it.'

'Yes, there was a reaction.'

'Well?'

'Nothing was said. They all went very, very quiet. But the two women certainly saw you. I could see the expressions on their faces. Then one of them nudged her husband.'

'You know, Paul, I think they're still watching us. I can feel four pairs of eyes boring into the back of my head. Can't you?'

'Silly cunts.'

'I'm sorry.'

'I suppose I should be used to it.'

'Shall we continue, Paul? Or – ?'

'Hmm?'

'Do you want to continue?'

'Oh. Oh, yes. To the end of the road. Which also happens to be the end of the village. Then we'll head back home. But, John, if you don't mind, let's drop the commentary for now. Let's walk in silence for a bit.'

'Righto.'

'Sorry.'

&

'What's that? Who *is* that?'

'Oh God, I'm terribly sorry. I didn't realize you were –'

'For Christ's sake, close the door!'

'Have you closed the door?'

'Yes, I have. Yes, it's closed.'

'Remember, not completely!'

'No, no. I remembered. Don't worry, I've left it slightly ajar. Look, Paul, I'm really, really sorry. I don't know what to say. The door was open so I assumed –'

'Well, I *did* tell you I always keep the bathroom door open. It was one of the first things I told you.'

'Yes, I know, but –'

'But nothing. I explained to you that it was a question of my claustrophobia. It makes no difference whether I'm taking a bath or a crap. It's distasteful, I know, but I did explain.'

'What I'm trying to say is that I assumed the bathroom was empty because the light was off.'

'What did you say?'

'I said the light was off.'

'The light was off? But the light's on. Of course it's on.'

'No, Paul, it's off. Look. Now I'm not opening the

door, so don't get alarmed. But I'm reaching in and pulling the cord now. There. Now it's on. On, off, on, off, on –'

'Yes, yes, yes, all right.'

'I don't understand. It's second nature to me. I *always* switch the light on when I enter the bathroom.'

'Maybe this time you forgot.'

'I never forget. But maybe, John, *you* forgot?'

'Me?'

'You went earlier, didn't you? Just before supper?'

'Uh, yes. Yes, I did.'

'Maybe you forgot to switch the light off.'

'Yes, it's possible. Yeah, that must have been what happened. If so, I really apologize. I know how strongly you feel about it.'

'I suppose it can't be helped. Actually, given my – my dishevelled state, it's maybe just as well the light was off.'

'Even so, I –'

'Yes, all right, you've already apologized. And this, you know, this is a quite *outstandingly* repellent conversation. You lurking behind the door, me plonked here with my trousers about my ankles. If you don't mind, I suggest we wrap it up at once. Give me five minutes and the bathroom's yours.'

'Thanks. But please don't rush on my account.'

'I won't. And we'll see each other in the morning. Goodnight, John.'

'Goodnight, Paul.'

❧

On reflection, and on the whole, I've decided that I like him. He's careless, even slapdash, he's not exactly literary and he's far from perfect – but then, one's unlikely to obtain perfection by advertising for it in the personal columns of a newspaper. Yet I feel certain he'll more than do. That mortifying business with me on thelav he handled well, all things considered. The omens are good.

❧

'Are you ready, John?'

'Yes, everything's ready. The Mac is humming away. I've created a new folder. I called it *Truth*.'

'*Truth*?'

'For *Truth and Consequences*? The full title would be too long.'

'I see. *Truth*, eh? Rather a lot to live up to, isn't it? But – well, it might be no bad thing at that. *Truth* it is.'

'Shall I date it?'

'Date it? Yes, why not? Write – let me see – write "Spring 1999".'

'"Spring 1999". Done. So – exactly how do we go about this?'

'Well, John, this is a book that's going to be very much about blindness, both literal and figurative, and I mean to begin it with a series of fragmented reflections on the subject. A kind of prelude.'

'Aha.'

'It's curious. Blindness was never one of my preoccupations, never one of my trademark themes. Ah well, that's life for you, I suppose. It will suddenly spring on you a climax for which nothing that's happened to you up to that point has prepared you.'

'Mmm.'

'Anyway, I intend the first of these reflections of mine to focus not only on blindness but on eyelessness. It strikes me that, with a book of this nature, in which narrative chronology is absolutely not at stake, there could be no stronger point of departure for the text. By the way, John?'

'Yes?'

'Did you make a note of that little felicity of mine, as I asked you?'

'Little felicity?'

'Comparing the moon to the title of a Japanese film?'

'Oh, God, no. No, I obviously didn't.'

'No, you obviously didn't. Here am I reminding you to remind me. Please note it now, will you, and don't forget the notebook if we go out for a stroll this evening.'

'Right. Though I'm not altogether out to lunch. This morning when I set up the Mac it occurred to me it might be useful to create a document called *Notes*. I'll just stick your felicity in it now. It won't take a sec.'

'Good idea. Keep that document handy for anything that comes up *en route*, so to speak. Sometimes, John, a writer has what may be described as a word-flow problem. It's exactly the same as a cash-flow problem, you know, only with words. It isn't that he's really short of words, I mean to say it isn't that he's *broke*, just that they aren't coming as smoothly as they ought. And sometimes consulting notes, even notes jotted down a long, long time before, ideas one's forgotten one ever had, will get the juices flowing again. I know what I'm talking about, I assure you. I speak from experience.'

'There. It's done.'

'Good. Now listen very carefully, John. I'm not going to pretend that what we're about to embark on, you and I, will be easy for either of us. It won't. I've never dictated my work before. You might say I was the kind of writer who felt most comfortable composing at the piano.'

'At the piano?'

'Metaphorically, John, metaphorically.'

'Ah.'

'I mean that I always used to write at the typewriter. Just as there are certain composers who would always compose at the piano – Stravinsky, for one, I seem to recall – because they found that just letting their fingers run over the keyboard would actually generate ideas – not just ideas but fully formed sentences that subsequently required next to no revision. I mean – of course, I don't mean that Stravinsky typed out *sentences* – I'm talking about writers, writers *like* Stravinsky, writers like me who were used to composing at a keyboard. Actually, when you think of it, there's – I mean, what I've just been saying, what I've just been struggling to say – there's a perfect example of what I'm talking about. If I'd seen that sentence coming, it wouldn't have been as abominably confused and unstructured as it actually turned out to be. Which – which is why – oh, forget it. Where was I?'

'You were saying you always composed at the typewriter.'

'Yes. So, now, since I'll no longer have direct access to a keyboard, and therefore to the idea of letters as objects, letters as individual objects, letters as hard, solid, buttony things that I can see and not only see but feel and touch and press, well, I'm going to need some time to adjust. Do you understand?'

'Yes, of course.'

'It's a bit like a smoker who's just given up smoking. The absence of nicotine is one thing – the essential thing, I imagine – I've never tried so I wouldn't know.

But there's also the absence of the cigarette itself, the cigarette between his fingers, the cigarette, if you like, as a *prop*. A smoker, John, a smoker without a cigarette between his fingers is like a courtesan without her gaudy rings.'

'Ah, yes. Quite witty.'

'It is, isn't it? I wonder if it's worth noting down. Unless –'

'Would you like me to make a note of it?'

'Well, finally, no. I fear I've used it before. In print, I mean. For the moment, I can't think precisely where or when, but I seem to – I'm sure – no, no, drop it. Don't bother.'

'Whatever you say.'

'Anyway, when I begin dictating, and even though I've had time to do a lot of thinking about this first section, it's liable to come out all higgledy-piggledy. Despite what you may think, I find I all too often, shall I say, stammer in my thoughts, and this stammering of mine, no matter how provisional, is something I'm going to find hard to live with. Except that there's nothing I can do about it so there's no point in complaining. But I do think it best if you just keep typing in what I say, including any minor revisions or refinements I make along the way – and for that matter they won't always be so very minor. Then, when we've finished a section, I can try to pull it all together into a more presentable shape.'

'That makes sense.'

'But please don't imagine that'll be the end of it. I intend to go over every passage again and again till not a semi-colon remains that I haven't vetted. You do understand? It's not easy being a blind perfectionist, but it's what I plan to be.'

'Well, Paul, since you put it that way . . .'

'Yes? What is it?'

'Look, this may be of no consequence, but I've noticed, well – I just thought –'

'Will you please say what it is you're trying to say.'

'I thought you'd want to know there's a stain on your tie.'

'A what?'

'A coffee stain. You splashed coffee on your tie at breakfast.'

'No? Oh God, I hate stains, I hate them! Even blind, I hate them! Oh dear, oh dear. Oh well – well, it's got to come off, obviously. Thank you for letting me know.'

'I wasn't sure if –'

'I didn't even mention stains to you – you know, when we talked earlier – because I'm usually very – I'm usually very fastidious about my personal manners. I pride myself – Oh dear. Oh well, it can't be helped. Here.'

'Oh. Right. Thanks.'

'Add it to the laundry. Later, when you make us some coffee. Can it be laundered, do you think?'

'Oh, yes. Probably.'

'I'm really steamed up about that tie. It's a Cerruti. As I recall, there were very few like it. With those velvety multicoloured squares.'

'What?'

'What?'

'You said multicoloured squares?'

'Yes?'

'Well, no.'

'What do you mean, no?'

'I mean there are no squares on it. It's actually brown, beigey-brown, with darker brown stripes. Diagonal stripes.'

'It's not the Cerruti?'

'The label says Stripes.'

'Stripes? Just Stripes?'

'Yeah.'

'But that's extraordinary. I have no such tie.'

'It's the tie you were wearing.'

'But I tell you it can't be.'

'Look, Paul, it's not important really, is it? After all, think about it. What it means is that you didn't stain the Cerruti, right? The tie you really liked?'

'You aren't listening. I don't possess a brown

striped tie. Repeat, I don't possess a brown striped tie. All my ties I purchased before I went blind and they're all laid out in order on a special hanger inside my wardrobe. I ought to know by now which is which. I simply don't recognize such a tie.'

'Well, I don't know what the answer is, but I'm sure it's nothing to get upset about. Later, if you like, I'll go over your ties with you and I guarantee you'll find everything in its place. Just for now, though, shouldn't we get started?'

'What? Oh. Yes, yes, of course. Forgive me. I'm so unused to – Yes, forgive me.'

'All right. All right, let's see. Uh, "I am blind."'
'Yes?'
'No, no, you don't understand. I want that to be the first sentence of the book.'
'Oh, I get it. Okay, here we go. "I am blind . . ." Full stop?'
'I said it was a sentence, didn't I? Don't bother with punctuation at the moment. Just go with your instincts.'
'Right.'

'Ready when you are, Paul.'
'And don't keep prompting me. It's counterproductive. When I have what I want to say, you'll be the first to know.'

'Sorry.'

'And for Christ's sake, don't keep saying you're sorry all the fucking time! It's driving me bananas!'

'Ah. Hmph. Now it's my turn to say sorry. My apologies, John. I'm just a little rattled this morning. That business of the tie. I can't imagine why it should have upset me as much as it has.'

'I repeat, my apologies.'

'Accepted.'

'I did tell you it wouldn't be easy. I'm not an easy man, I know it.'

'It's fine, it's fine. Don't worry.'

'Good. Then let's proceed. "I am blind. I have no sight. Equally I have no eyes." Tell me if I'm going too fast.'

'That's okay as it is.'

'"Equally I have no eyes. I am thus a freak. For blindness is freakish, is surreal."'

'Sorry. Do you want both "is freakish" and "is surreal"?'

'Yes, I do: "is freakish", comma, "is surreal", full stop. "For blindness is freakish, is surreal." No, that's terrible – it's – oh God, this won't do.'

'Look, John, forget what I just said. Just go on whether it's terrible or not. Don't listen to any of my complaints. Keep typing away whatever I say. Use your judgement.'

'Right.'

'"Even more surreal" – I'm dictating now, by the way – "even more surreal than my blindness itself, however, is the fact that, without any eyes to see" – no, "is the fact that, having been dispossessed not only of my sight but of my eyes, I continue to see" – inverted commas around "to see" – no, on second thoughts, only around the word "see" – "I continue to 'see' nevertheless. What it is that I see" – naturally, there are no inverted commas this time – "what it is that I see may be 'nothing'" – inverted commas again.'

'For "nothing"?'

'Yes. "What it is that I see may be 'nothing'" – dash – "I am blind, after all" – dash – "but that 'nothing'" – keep the inverted commas – "is, paradoxically, by no means indescribable" – no, "is, paradoxically, by no means beyond my powers of description. I see nothing, yet, amazingly, I am able to describe that nothing. The world for me, the world of sightlessness, has become a sombre and coarsely textured plaid" – that's plaid as in a Scotch plaid – "as devoid of light as I imagine deep space must be and yet somehow, also like deep space, penetrable. And, I repeat, I really do see it. There would seem to exist a profound impulse" – no, "an immemorial impulse" – no, wait, "a profound and immemorial impulse" – yes, "a profound and immemorial impulse in that part of my face where my eyes used to be to 'look out'" – inverted commas around "look out". Actually, from now on I'll say "ICs" for inverted commas. I tend to use them a lot in my prose. Where was I?'

'"There would seem to be a profound and immemorial impulse –"'

'I think you'll find I said "would seem to *exist* a profound and immemorial impulse –"'

'"There would seem to exist a profound and immemorial impulse in that part of my face where my eyes used to be –"'

'Comma – "in that part of my face where my eyes used to be" – matching comma – "to 'look out' at the world, an impulse that, even when I no longer have eyes" – I fear I'm being repetitive here but we'll tidy it up later – "even when I no longer have eyes, does not then spread indiscriminately to the rest of my face. It is still with my missing eyes, exclusively with them, that I see nothing" – ICs around "see nothing". "I still turn my head to greet someone, not merely in unthinking obeisance" – o, b, e, i, s, a, n, c, e – "not merely in unthinking obeisance to the weary conventions of casual social intercourse." No, let's say rather "jejune social intercourse". I don't want "casual" next to "social".'

'Why not?'

'Too elly.'

'Too elly?'

'Too many l's. "Casual", "social". It's practically a rhyme. I don't need it.'

'Okay. Sorry, but how do you spell "jejune"?'

'J, e, j, u, n, e.'

'To be honest, I've never known what that word means.'

'*You* don't have to know what it means. I'm going on. So – "blah blah blah not merely in unthinking obeisance to the weary conventions of jejune social intercourse but also as though, even eyeless, I remain under the sway of an instinctual and atavistic seeing reflex. In short, I continue to see" – ICs, please – "the same plaid, the same deep space, because as a human being I cannot not see it" – semi-colon – "because seeing is a function of the organism even when the organs themselves have been removed. I have to see –" Better underline "have".'

'You mean, italicize it?'

'Can do you that?'

'Yes, of course.'

'On the computer screen?'

'Absolutely. I've done it already.'

'Good Lord. What a dream machine it must be. I almost wish I could see it. Well, never mind. Read that last bit back to me, please.'

'The last bit. "I continue to 'see' the same plaid, the same deep space, because as a human being I cannot not see it; because seeing is a function of the organism even when the organs themselves have been removed. I *have* to see –"'

'"I *have* to see, whether such is my active intention or not. It is an itch which scratches itself, an itch comparable to that which makes amputees worry over" – no, "fret over" – "fret over their missing limbs. For there is, seemingly, what might be called an etiquette of amputation, an Emily Postish" – that's "Emily Post" plus "ish", one word, no hyphen, please – "an Emily Postish list of dos and don'ts where the physically impaired are concerned, mostly don'ts, of course. Thus, one should not sit on an amputee's bed at the exact spot where his leg would normally be, one should not violate the – the air space of his missing arm, etc."'

'Do you want me to write "etc"?'

'Just the usual abbreviation, please. Are you getting all this?'

'Think so. But, tell me, we're still on the same paragraph, right?'

'Yes. Well, actually, no. Now I think of it, no. New paragraph coming up. I'll tell you when in future.'

'Okay. New paragraph. Go on.'

'Go on! Go on! Easy to say.'

'Or don't go on, as the case may be.'

'"The question" – I'm going on – "the question is more general, however, than that posed by blindness alone. In my own past, whenever an optician or ophthalmologist trained a torch" – no, a – a – a – what are they called, those slim little torches that opticians use?'

'A pencil torch?'

'A pencil torch, yes. "In the past –"'

'"In *my own* past –"'

'"In my own past, whenever an optician or ophthalmologist trained a pencil torch on my eye, or whenever I myself chanced to rub too hard and long on my eyeball, I seemed to catch sight of" – dash – "well, what precisely?" Don't forget the question mark. "Well, what precisely? The retina? The eyeball's inner surface? Its outer surface? Whichever" – colon – "cratered, cicatrized, lunar" – comma – "as raw" – no, wait, better underline "lunar".'

'Right. Is "cicatrized" spelt with an s or a z?'

'Who cares? That's the sort of thing we can fix up later. "Whichever: cratered, cicatrized, *lunar*, as red and rawly textured as the skin of a scrawny day-old nestling, as biliously opaque as a – as a gaudy glass paperweight, the sight of it was deeply disquieting. It reminded me of the earth's primaeval convulsions in the horrendously vulgar *Sacre du Printemps* sequence of Walt Disney's *Fantasia*" – wait, cut "horrendously vulgar", this isn't a work of film criticism – "in the

Sacre du Printemps sequence of Walt Disney's *Fantasia*. It reminded me, above all, that the eyes are two parts of the body, are things" – italicize – "*things*, units that can be lost, broken, cracked –"'

'Shouldn't that be "lost, cracked, broken"?'

'Oh. And why?'

'Just that there appears to be an ascending order of seriousness and "cracked" is surely less serious than "broken"?'

'Quite right, quite right. Well spotted, John. Keep taking the tablets.'

'We aim to please.'

'I'm going on: "that can be lost, cracked, broken, that, as I well know, can be disjoined from the head and held, even rolled around, in the palm of the hand. From inside my head" – ICs around "inside" – "from 'inside' my head it never occurred to me, unless I happened to think of it" – ICs around "think of it" – "that I had in reality two eyes, not one. From inside I was a human Cyclops" – capital C, semi-colon – "my Cyclops eye, as I perceived it, was both the spectator and screen of the world" – semi-colon – "the world, as I confronted and controlled it – I mean, attempted to control it" – that "I mean" is in the text, incidentally, after a dash – "was in a tangible sense inside the eye" – open brackets – "(remove the eye and you also remove the world)" – close brackets, full stop. "The eye, then, was finally just that glass paperweight which I mention above – " Wait, though, wait. Did I?'

'Did you what?'

'Mention a glass paperweight?'

'Bubbubbubbubbubbubbubbubbub. Yes, you did: "as biliously opaque as a gaudy glass paperweight".'

'Of course I did. I'm going on. "The eye, then, was finally just that gaudy glass paperweight which I mention above, save that, instead of a nostalgic little Christmassy vista" – open brackets – "(soft snow falls if you hold it upside-down)" – close brackets – "what it contained was the world itself." New paragraph. "But was I really seeing it" – ICs around "seeing", comma after "it" – "was I really seeing my own eye? How can an eye manage to see itself? See inwardly or, so to speak, self-referentially? Even way back then, I was myopic, even then I saw the external world only with glasses. Yet, miraculously, I could see this lunar surface just as sharply as would anyone possessed of normal vision. What was it, though, that I saw it with" – underline "with", question mark. "What was it, though, that I saw it *with*? With, doubtless, that instinctual and atavistic seeing reflex that I have already referred to and that ultimately transcends the possession of one's very organs of sight."'

'Paul? Would you like to stop for a moment?'

'Why do you ask?'

'You seem a bit distracted.'

'I told you how hard it would be for me to dictate a book. It is. Harder than I dreamed. I'm sweating like a pig. My shirt's damp at the collar. Why am I sweating so?'

'Shall we take a short break? Elevenses?'

'Yes. Yes, John, it might be a good idea to take a break. Though, if we're to finish within the year, we can't take too many of them.'

'True. But will I get us some coffee now?'

'Did it all appear to make sense to you?'

'To be honest, Paul, I was too busy taking it down to take it in.'

'Well, I'm sorry, but I've got to know the worst. Read it back to me, will you.'

'Everything, you mean?'

'From the top, as cocktail pianists say. Slowly and fluently. And no matter what I think of it, no matter if I die a little on hearing it, I promise not to interrupt. Then we'll have our break. Deal?'

'Deal. All right, here we go. "I am blind. I have no sight. Equally –"'

'Not so fast.'

'Sorry. Okay. "I am blind. I have no sight. Equally I have no eyes. I am thus a freak. For blindness is freakish, is surreal."'

'Oh God, it's so jerky. So many short sentences. It's like a leader in the *Daily Express*.'

'Paul, you promised not to interrupt.'

'I'm sorry, it's just so simplistic.'

'You'll have plenty of time later to complicate it.'

'Hmm. I'll take that in the spirit in which I trust it was intended. All right, go on. I won't say another word.'

'"I am blind. I have no sight. Equally I have no eyes. I am thus a freak. For blindness is freakish, is surreal. Even more surreal than my blindness itself, however, is the fact that, having been dispossessed not only of my sight but of my eyes, I continue to 'see' nevertheless. What it is that I see may be 'nothing' – I am blind, after all – but that 'nothing' is, paradoxically, by no means beyond my powers of description. I see nothing, yet, amazingly, I am able to describe that nothing. The world for me, the world of sightlessness, has become a sombre and coarsely textured plaid as devoid of light as I imagine deep space must be and yet somehow, also like deep space, penetrable. And, I repeat, I really do see it. There would seem to exist a profound and immemorial impulse, in that part of my face where my eyes used to be, to 'look out' at the world, an impulse that, even when I no longer have eyes, does not then spread indiscriminately to the rest of my face. It is still with my missing eyes, exclusively

-73-

with them, that I 'see nothing'. I still turn my head to greet someone, not merely in unthinking obeisance to the weary conventions of jejune social intercourse but also as though, even eyeless, I remain subject to an instinctual and atavistic seeing reflex. In short, I continue to 'see' the same plaid, the same deep space, because as a human being I cannot not see it; because seeing is a function of the organism even when the organs themselves have been removed. I *have* to see, whether such is my active intention or not. It is an itch which scratches itself, an itch comparable to that which makes amputees fret over their missing limbs. For there is, seemingly, what might be called an etiquette of amputation, an Emily Postish list of dos and don'ts where the physically impaired are concerned, mostly don'ts, of course. Thus, one should not sit on an amputee's bed at the exact spot where his leg would normally be, one should not violate the air space of his missing arm, etc.

'"The question is more general, however, than that posed by blindness alone. In my own past, whenever an optician or ophthalmologist trained a pencil torch on my eye, or whenever I myself chanced to rub too hard and long on my eyeball, I seemed to catch sight of – well, what precisely? The retina? The eyeball's inner surface? Its outer surface? Whichever: cratered, cicatrized, *lunar*, as red and rawly textured as the skin of a scrawny day-old nestling, as biliously opaque as a gaudy glass paperweight, the sight of it was deeply disquieting. It reminded me of the earth's primaeval convulsions in the *Sacre du Printemps* sequence of Walt Disney's *Fantasia*. It reminded me, above all, that the eyes are two parts of the body, are *things*, units that can be lost, cracked, broken, that, as I well know, can be disjoined from the head and held, even rolled around, in the palm of the hand. From 'inside' my head it never occurred to me, unless I happened to 'think of it', that I had in reality two eyes, not one. From inside I was a human Cyclops; my Cyclops eye, as I perceived it, was both the spectator and screen of the world; the world, as I confronted and controlled it – I mean, attempted to control it – was in a tangible sense inside the eye (remove the eye and you also remove the world). The eye, then, was finally just that gaudy glass paperweight which I mention above, save that, instead of a nostalgic little Christmassy vista (soft snow falls if you hold it upside-down), what it contained was the world itself.

'"But was I really 'seeing' it, was I really seeing my own eye? How can an eye manage to see itself? See inwardly or, so to speak, self-referentially? Even way back then, I was myopic, even then I saw the external world only with glasses. Yet, miraculously, I could see this lunar surface just as sharply as would anyone possessed of normal vision. What was it, though, that I saw it *with*? With, doubtless, that instinctual and atavistic seeing reflex that I have already referred to and that ultimately transcends the possession of one's very organs of sight."'

'Sorry to be a bore, John, but I want to add something. Directly following "I *have* to see, whether such is my active intention or not", I want to add – in brackets – something along the lines of "Let the reader close his eyes and verify for himself that, even then, even with his eyes closed, he continues to see" – inverted commas around "see" – "even if what he sees is nothing at all" – close brackets.'

'You want me to add that now?'

'Yes, I do.'

'Very well. Can you dictate it again? More slowly this time.'

'"Let the reader close his eyes –"'

'Hold on, I've got to find the place.'

'Right. Fire away.'

'"Let the reader close his eyes –"'

'Sorry.'

'What is it now?'

'You don't want to say, "Let the reader close his or her eyes"?'

'Lord, no! I told you once before I won't be a slave to that PC poppycock. It becomes so infernally awkward. "Let the reader close his *or her* eyes and verify for himself *or herself* –"'

'Okay, okay. "And verify for *him*self –" Go on.'

'"And verify for himself that, even then, even with his eyes tightly closed, he continues to see" – ICs – "even if what he sees is nothing at all."'

'Close brackets?'

'Close brackets. Shit, I've suddenly realized. Three "evens" in the same sentence. And I shudder to think how you spelt *Sacre du Printemps*. Never mind, we'll have another look at it all after we've had our break. I wonder how long it is. Offhand, I'd say just under eight hundred words. Seven hundred and – oh, fifty.'

'Give me a sec and I'll have the exact figure for you.'

'What? Don't tell me you're some kind of mathematical prodigy? What do they call them? Idiot savants?'

'No, of course not. I'm getting the Mac to give me a word count.'

'Curiouser and curiouser. Is there anything it can't do?'

'Not much. Here you are. Seven hundred and seventy-five words. Not counting the title and date, seven hundred and seventy.'

'Seven hundred and seventy, eh?'

'I must say, you made a very impressive guess.'

'When you've been around words for as long as I have, you get an instinct for these things.'

'So, Paul? Pleased with it?'

'I don't know what I think. This afternoon I may decide to cut the whole passage.'

'What!'

'Just kidding, John, just kidding. But be warned nevertheless. Somewhere along the line, and more than once, that's exactly what *will* happen. If the reader skips any of the pages of a book, it's almost always because the author himself should have skipped. That witticism – whose was it? Oscar Wilde's? Flaubert's? – the one about spending an entire morning putting a comma in and an entire afternoon taking it out again is no joke. You'll just have to learn to live with it, as I have.'

'I'm sure I'll take it in my stride. Meanwhile, what about coffee? Unless you'd prefer something stronger. A glass of wine, maybe?'

'No, no, no. Coffee it's got to be. A writer never drinks and writes. It's as dangerous as drinking and driving.'

'Really? What about Hemingway? What about Charles Bukowski?'

'Bukowski's rubbish.'

'And Hemingway?'

'Is he the sort of writer you think I am, John? Gutsy?

Hard-boiled? Whisky-swigging?'

'I'll make the coffee.'

∾

'Well?'

'God, this is a roomy wardrobe. You could actually step inside it.'

'I'm aware of that. What about the ties?'

'Quite an array of them here.'

'Yes, all right. But is the Cerruti among them?'

'Sorry. Describe it to me again.'

'Velvet. With a motif of coloured squares. And the label's Cerruti. Or Cerruti 1880. Or 1885. Something like that, I forget. That's C, e, r, r, u, t, i.'

'I'll go through them one by one, shall I? No. No. No. No. No. No. Oh, here's a Cerruti! No, this one has a spiral design. Nice tie, though.'

'Really, John, I wish you'd keep your mind on the job.'

'I am keeping my mind on the job.'

'No, you aren't. And I understand. But what *you* must understand is that the tie itself isn't ultimately what matters. Since the accident – I mean, since I began to get my act together, as they say – I've learned to manoeuvre myself through the labyrinth of the world – because, you know, for me the world *is* a labyrinth – without either of my eyes. But if for any reason that world is tampered with, I simply cannot function. I simply can't. So, for example, Old Ma Kilbride knows that whenever she does the cleaning she's got to put every chair, every lamp, every bloody toothpick, back precisely where she found it. Not a centimetre to the left or right. Otherwise, you see, I really *am* blind.'

'Well, Paul, I'm sorry to say that, while you've been talking, I've examined all the ties in the wardrobe and the only Cerruti is the one I mentioned already. I'm sorry.'

'Why, that's – that's really most extraordinary. I don't know what to believe.'

'Could Mrs Kilbride have taken it to the laundry without telling you?'

'Don't be ridiculous. I've just told you. She won't touch anything, anything at all, without first getting my permission.'

'Well then, could it have been stolen?'

'Stolen? A Cerruti tie? Preposterous. Who would have stolen it? No one ever comes here except Mrs Kilbride and – you've yet to meet him, I know – but the mind fairly boggles at the notion of Joe Kilbride mucking out his byre in a Cerruti tie. Of course it hasn't been stolen. Not on the wardrobe floor, is it?'

'I've already looked.'

'Or else slipped behind – behind I don't know what?'

'Nope.'

'Extraordinary, really extraordinary. Really rather unsettling. I feel as though I've tried to cash one of God's cheques and it's bounced.'

'Oh, and John, don't bother jotting that one down. I've used it before. I've used it many times before.'

∾

Where is that tie? Where is it? It's absurd to be unnerved by something so insignificant, but if just one brick is removed I have the impression the whole edifice is about to collapse on top of me. I simply can't bear not knowing things. It forces me to realize that, for all my boasting and bragging, I was not observant at all. It forces me to realize how little I ever did look about me, how heartrendingly little of the world I ever truly saw. I didn't have to look at things, I didn't have to see them, they were there. Now nothing at all is there unless and until I know it's there, and this one trivial enigma makes me wonder how much I think is there that no longer is. Oh God.

∾

'Here you are, Paul.'
    'Neat?'
    'Naturally.'
    'Chin chin.'

'Chin chin.'

'You know, John.'

'Yes?'

'Having you here is just about the best thing that could have happened to me.'

'Nice of you to say so.'

'I mean it. Even aside from the work.'

'Well, thank you. I appreciate that.'

'And you? Do you enjoy being here? Please be honest.'

'Yes, I do. It's as stimulating as I hoped it would be.'

'It *is* going well, don't you think?'

'I'd say so. But I can only speak for myself. I don't know how much you'd normally expect to get done in nine days.'

'Oh, well, as for that, rather more than you and I have done. But you must realize, my fear was that I wouldn't be able to work at all under these conditions. Yet we *have* worked together well, haven't we?'

'Yes, we have.'

'Worked surprisingly well, right?'

'Absolutely.'

'I haven't been too – too martinettish with you?'

'Too what?'

'Too much the martinet.'

'You warned me, Paul.'

'Well, hell, that means I have, doesn't it?'

'No. No, it doesn't, actually. Look, you're hardly the easiest person in the world to get along with. I'd be a liar if I tried to pretend you were. But, as I say, in the first place you did warn me.'

'And in the second place?'

'Well, uh, actually, there is no second place.'

'Ah. And here was I hoping you'd say that in the second place it's a privilege for you to be allowed to collaborate on this book of mine. My last book and, I believe, my best.'

'Paul, that went without saying.'

'Ah. Thank you. Well now. What's today?'

'Friday.'

'Friday. So it is. That means, I suppose, you're off tomorrow?'

'Yes, I do have to get back to town.'

'It isn't a problem, is it, Paul? I mean, it *was* agreed I'd be returning at the weekend?'

'Oh, absolutely.'

'I'll probably get going just after –'

'I *was* wondering, though.'

'Yes?'

'Of course I don't know just how busy you're planning to be?'

'Pretty busy, I expect. I haven't been home for more than a week. There'll be mail to answer, e-mail, faxes, the usual sort of thing. What was it you were going to ask me?'

'Well, if you had a couple of hours to kill – mind you, only if you really did have a couple of hours –'

'I probably will.'

'There's a reconnoitring job I shall want you to do for the next section of the book. And if you did it over the weekend, you see, it would save you driving back up to London on Monday or Tuesday.'

'What exactly would it involve?'

'There are two jobs, but they're both in the same area. Next door to each other, in fact.'

'Why don't you just tell me what it is you want me to do?'

'In the National Gallery there's a Rembrandt self-portrait. Actually, there are two of them, but the one I'm talking about is my very favourite painting in the world. I mean to write about it in this new section that we're now going to be tackling. Briefly, it'll have to do with the whole concept of self-portraiture, particularly if you're blind. I intend to call it "The Melancholy of Anatomy".'

'Uh huh.'

'Well, that went down like a lead balloon.'

'Sorry, what?'

'Oh, nothing. Anyway, my thesis, which I'm about to simplify grossly, is that all the great self-portraits were painted as though by blind men and – God, it sounds frightfully trite put like that, but maybe you get the picture?'

'I think so. And you want me to – ?'

'What I need is a meticulously detailed description of that particular self-portrait. It's the older of the two in the National. I mean, in actual fact it's the more recent, it's Rembrandt himself who's older, visibly older. If I remember aright, it was painted just days before he died. There ought to be a postcard of it for sale in the souvenir shop. In which case, buy it and bring it back with you. Otherwise, I'll need you to study the painting and make notes of every detail. You understand? So I can copy it. A bit like an art student installing himself in front of the portrait and painting a copy. Only, in my case, in words.'

'Yes, I can do that.'

'Now I think of it, even if you do manage to find a postcard, it'll still be better if you take some time to study the painting itself. Get a sense of the brush-strokes. It should take no more than half an hour out of your weekend.'

'Not a problem.'

'I'd also like – don't ask – but I'd also like you to see if you could purchase, again in the souvenir shop, a jigsaw puzzle of the Rembrandt.'

'A jigsaw puzzle?'

'I know you can buy jigsaw puzzles of some of the paintings in the National's collection. Holbein's "Ambassadors" is definitely one. Probably Seurat's "Bathers". Oh, and the Crivelli "Annunciation with Saint Emidius". I seriously doubt there'll be one of the Rembrandt. Who'd want to do a jigsaw puzzle of a bulbous-nosed old codger in a smock? But will you take a look nevertheless?'

'Was that the second favour?'

'No, that's still the first. The second – well, just in front of the National Gallery there is of course Trafalgar Square. And, as you probably know, there are three statues at three out of its four corners. I mean, apart from Nelson's Column. At the corners, not in the middle.'

'Yes, of course. I know those statues. There *are* only three of them, not four, right?'

'Exactly. Well – and again, don't ask – but I want you to report back with two pieces of factual data relating to those statues. First, which out of the four is the empty plinth? Is it the top right-hand corner one or else the bottom left-hand –'

'I think I already know the answer to that. Isn't it at the top left-hand corner?'

'I wouldn't be asking you if I could remember myself. Just double-check it, will you. It's for a book, not a dinner-party conversation. It's got to be absolutely right.'

'Right.'

'Second, who are the other statues of? The three names. One of them, I'm fairly sure, is George IV. The others, if I ever knew who they were, I no longer remember. And again, of course, who's actually standing on which plinth?'

'That's all?'

'That's it. You see, it would take just one trip to Trafalgar Square. But, as I said before, only if it won't spoil your weekend.'

'No, no. I'm going to be around and about anyway. And it'll be good for me. I haven't been to the National Gallery in years.'

'Then when shall I see you?'

'Well, I expect to leave just after breakfast tomorrow and return Sunday evening or first thing Monday morning. That okay?'

'That's perfect. Because I'll want you to help me make a phone call Monday morning. I'd like to ring up my agent.'

'No problem. I'll most likely get back on Sunday evening. But very late. Don't wait up for me. I'll let myself in.'

'Yes, all right.'

'There's one other thing, Paul.'

'Yes?'

'You think I might have a cheque before I go?'

'A cheque?'

'Well, yes.'

'But I thought we agreed that, at least to start with, you wouldn't be paid in advance? Not till we were both quite sure of each other?'

'For the computer. You haven't paid me for the computer yet.'

'The computer? Haven't I? Good Lord, you're right. I've been so engrossed in the book I completely forgot the computer. Oh dear, how very remiss of me. Of course I'll give you a cheque, I'll give it to you right now, if you like. But will you be able to deposit it? On a Saturday, I mean?'

'Well, no.'

'Well, then?'

'If I return Monday morning I can deposit it first thing at a bank in Chipping Campden.'

'But you said you'd most likely be returning on Sunday?'

'In that case, I'll simply mail it to my own branch of Barclays over the weekend.'

'Can you do that?'

'Oh yes.'

'Well, of course I'll give you a cheque. My cheque-book's in the drawer of my escritoire. The top drawer. If you could just –'

'Here you are.'

'Thank you, John.'

∽

Nine days. Nine days already. Do I still remember my life, my quotidian round, as it was before John arrived? Well, for heaven's sake, of course I do! Even so, even so, it'll be hard for me to pick up that life again when he's no longer part of it. I was always a loner, yes, it's true, but a loner is someone who chooses to be alone – and chooses less to be alone than to be left alone. There's all the difference in the world between being alone and wishing to be left alone, the difference, per-haps, between meting out to a masochist the unique brand of pain, the unique specialty, which he craves and just plain hurting him. Oh well, early days yet.

∽

'Jazz! Jazz! Jazz!

'Oh, give me no Creole cookery,
No dinner at Antoine's, no Vieux Carré!
What I want is a hosanna,
A blast of Armstrongiana
From old Louisianaaaa
's favorite son Louis!

'Jazz! Jazz! Jazz!

'Now the music sounds Scarlattian
On the island of Manhattian
Where the rhythms are blasé
And bluesy and jazzy
And razzamatazzy
Like the "Rhapsody in Blu-é"!

'Jazz! Ja –'

'Hello?'

'Who is it?'

'Who is that? Is someone there?'

'Is that you, Ryder?'

'John? Is that you? Are you there? Is someone there?'

∾

'Good morning, Paul. Sleep well?'
    'No, I didn't.'
    'I'm sorry to hear that. I hope I didn't wake you
coming in? I tried to be as quiet as I could.'
    'Tell me. Just when did you come in?'

'Late. After midnight. Closer to one. I had dinner with a friend in Notting Hill, then drove straight down here afterwards.'

'So you weren't back about eleven?'

'Eleven? Eleven last night?'

'Of course, eleven last night! What other eleven could I possibly be talking about?'

'Well, don't bite my head off. I told you not to bother waiting up.'

'I didn't wait up. Oh look, I – I'm sorry, John. I'm very rattled this morning. I had a rather eerie experience.'

'Why, what happened?'

'Nothing. It's too silly for words.'

'Tell me what happened.'

'Let's just drop it, shall we? I was probably imagining things. I do sometimes. Did you manage to get the information I asked you for?'

'I got the postcard. I bought three of them, just in case. And the jigsaw puzzle.'

'The jigsaw puzzle? Of Rembrandt's self-portrait?'

'Yeah.'

'Really? You amaze me.'

'It was on sale alongside the others you mentioned.'

'Well, that *is* a windfall. I fully expected to have to ask you to improvise – to have you cut a jigsaw-shaped piece out of one of the postcards.'

'Sorry, I'm not with you on this. You remember, you

never did tell me what the jigsaw puzzle was going to be for? Would you like me to refill your cup, by the way?'

'Thanks. A dab of sugar with this one, if you don't mind.'

'Sure thing.'

'Here you are. Now. The jigsaw puzzle?'

'Oh well, it's the sort of thing that may or may not work. But I wanted you – or rather, I *want* you, since you unexpectedly did come up trumps – I want you to put the puzzle together except for the pieces where the eyes are. You know, a self-portrait without eyes? Something along those lines.'

'I see.'

'As I say, it may work. What about Trafalgar Square?'

'Ah, now that *was* interesting.'

'Yes?'

'Well, I had no difficulty finding the identities of the three statues. Hold on. I've got my notes somewhere. Unless you'd prefer to wait till after breakfast?'

'Please. If you've got your notes on you, read them to me now.'

'Here they are. They're a bit rumpled but legible. All right. At the top right-hand corner of Trafalgar Square the statue, as you guessed, is of George IV.'

'Uh huh.'

'Bottom right-hand corner is one Major-General Sir

Henry Havelock, K. C. B., whatever that stands for. King's something, I suppose. King's Cross?'

'Don't know. Go on.'

'There's a quotation from him inscribed on the plinth, dating from the Indian Campaign of 1857. Would you like to hear it?'

'I suppose so.'

'"Soldiers!"'

'Please, John, I've told you before. You don't know the power of your own voice.'

'Sorry. "Soldiers. Your Labours Your Privations Your Sufferings and Your Valour will not be forgotten by a Grateful Country".'

'Peuh! Note how he rates privations and sufferings over valour. Typical military slimeball. Probably a bloodthirsty butcher.'

'Lower left-hand corner is Charles James Napier. That name seems to mean something.'

'Another general.'

'Really? I'd have said a scientist. His dates were MDCCLXXXII to MDCCCLIII. If you like, I can work them out for you.'

'Don't bother. So, as you thought, the unoccupied plinth is the top left-hand corner one?'

'Ah but, Paul, that's what's interesting. It only goes to show how out of touch you can get even when you aren't –'

'What's interesting about it?'

'It's no longer unoccupied.'

'What!'

'I'd vaguely heard that plans had been mooted, but I'd no idea they'd already been carried out.'

'What *are* you talking about?'

'They've erected a new statue on it.'

'A statue? Of whom?'

'Who do you think?'

'John, I'm in no mood, or condition, for guessing games.'

'Diana!'

'Who?'

'Diana. Princess Diana? You know, she was killed in an accident in Paris? About eighteen months ago?'

'Yes, thank you, John, I *was* aware of Diana's death. I'm blind, not deaf. Even I have to take notice when the entire cosmos weeps. But what are you telling me? That there's now a statue of Diana in Trafalgar Square?'

'That's right.'

'But that's unbelievable. How could such a monstrosity have been permitted?'

'I believe they held some sort of nationwide poll – what are they called? – a referendum – and Diana was way ahead of the field.'

'Well!'

'You know, John, this has come as quite a shock to me. I'm starting to wonder whether I'm actually cut out to be a hermit.'

'It must have happened very quickly. Even I didn't know.'

'What's it like?'

'The statue? I'm afraid it *is* something of a monstrosity. Head held high, hair streaming in the wind, skirt billowing around her legs. And she's holding a baby in her arms.'

'One of her own?'

'Own what?'

'Babies, man, babies! Is it one of her own offspring? Or some kind of African baby?'

'Ah, well, African, I'd say. Or Indian. The image is very much Diana the angel of mercy. Mother Diana of Calcutta.'

'Well, well, well. That rather puts the kibosh on my little conceit.'

'What conceit was that?'

'Oh, I thought I might get some symbolic mileage out of the empty plinth. Probably just as well it's been filled. It risked being intolerably pretentious.'

'Look, Paul –'

'Yes?'

'Well . . . Well, shoot this idea down if you think it silly.'

'I will.'

'But, well, couldn't you do something instead with the symbolism of Diana's statue?'

'What do you mean?'

'The accident . . . the car crash . . . the fact that both you and she . . .'

'Why, John, you may just have something there.'

'Thanks. I was worried you might find it –'

'It wouldn't be too crass, do you think? No, I don't see why. Not the way I'd handle it. Fact, it might even be rather haunting. And – and yes, of course! – I can finally place that article I wrote that they never used.'

'Sorry, what article?'

'A piece about the whole Diana cult that I wrote a few years back. Arsehole editor of the *Sunday Times* turned it down because it was too "literary". Naturally, it was literary! Why in heaven's name commission me at all unless you expect to get literature!'

'John?'

'Sorry. I was thinking of something.'

'You know, John, when you're in the company of a blind man, you've got to take care not to fall silent too often. The blind take silences extremely seriously. They interpret each one – each silence, I mean – just the way you, for example, might interpret a stray remark at a dinner table. "What exactly did he mean by that?" you think. And it nags at you all the evening. And you lie awake in bed worrying at it. Well, for a blind man, silence is just like that. Sometimes – in fact, too bloody frequently – Charles, my dear friend Charles, would abruptly fall silent when we were out on a stroll together and we actually had rows, quite serious rows, when I tried to get him to tell me what was on his mind.'

'I've no objection to telling you what's on mine.'

'I'm listening.'

'It's just that I was shocked when you said you were thinking of using a piece you'd already written.'

'Shocked? Heavens, why were you shocked?'

'Well. Well, I've come to think of this – what we've been working on – as your most personal book, a book written out of your pain, out of your solitude, your –'

'Yes, yes. Get on with it, man.'

'Now you've decided to put something in it you've done before. Well, with respect, that strikes me as a bit cynical, somehow.'

'I must say, John, I'm touched by your naïveté.'

'You think I'm naïve?'

'I think it's sweet that you have so romantically high-minded a view of the literary vocation. Much, though, as I hate to destroy your illusions, I have to tell you that we writers are the most environmentally friendly creatures you could ever imagine. We're constantly looking for ways of recycling our work.'

'Serving up as brand new something you wrote years ago? Isn't that cheating the public?'

'The public? Who are they? What do they know? The idea the public has of the birth of a work of literature is exactly comparable, *exactly comparable*, to that which infants have of the birth of a baby. Most people think books are brought by the stork.'

'Pardon me, Paul. But why do I have the feeling you've said that before?'

'Really, John, this is too much. As I recall, there was nothing in my advertisement about the suitable candidate being required to advise me on how to write my own book.'

'I'm sorry, I didn't mean to be rude. But a few of my past suggestions you *have* found helpful.'

'Is it acknowledgement you want? Do you want me to insert a footnote crediting you with the Diana idea? Which, frankly, I'm starting to think is just not worth the hassle.'

'Very well, Paul, I won't say another word. I'll just take dictation like the secretary you hired me to be.'

'Now don't go all sulky on me, please. As I said, as I

have said, John, I'm delighted with our collaboration, really delighted. In this instance, however, I can't help feeling you've overstepped the bounds of what you should or should not feel free to say.'

'It won't happen again, I assure you.'

'Oh please. *Please*. No huffs. I can't bear them. Let's just forget it happened at all. And actually, John, actually, on reflection I have to say you're right. There. I've admitted it.'

'Right about what?'

'For a book like this, it's true, I shouldn't be using something second-hand. It *is* cynical. Not just cynical but defeatist. And the tone of the article would be all wrong. Too journalistic, too "topical". You're quite right. If I don't have anything new to say, I ought not to be writing such a book. So will you accept my apologies? Yet again?'

'Of course I accept.'

'Good. Now. I think I told you the other day I wanted you to help me ring up my agent. I haven't spoken to Andrew in an age. Naturally, I haven't told him anything about the new book. Or about you. We've rather lost touch, he and I.'

'Ah. So you can't make telephone calls by yourself?'

'Mrs Kilbride usually makes them for me. Not that there are many these days. Would you mind dialling for me?'

'Not at all.'

The number is 631.3341. His name is Andrew Boles. And, John, before you dial –'

'Yes?'

'I'll speak only to Andrew himself. No secretaries, please. If he's not in, just ring off.'

'Right.'

'Another thing. Don't tell him it's me.'

'Don't tell him it's you? Who am I supposed to say it is?'

'It's been so long since we've spoken I imagine he's forgotten all about me, quite written me off. I'd like the call to be a surprise. Whether it's likely to be a pleasant surprise or not is another matter.'

'Oh, I see. Okay. Sorry, what was that number again?'

'6, 3, 1.'

'Yes?'

'3, 3, 4, 1.'

'Ringing.'

'Hello? Yes, could I speak to Andrew Boles, please?'

'Yes, hello. I wonder if I could speak to Andrew Boles, please?'

'Oh, he is? Can you tell me for how long?'

'I see.'

'No. No, I'll call again when he's back. Thanks anyway.'

'Bye.'

'He's out?'
'Away.'
'Away? Where?'
'The Far East. Hong Kong, Australia, then back home by way of San Francisco and New York. He'll be gone at least another fortnight.'
'Ah. Oh well. At least it means the book will have a real existence when we finally do talk. Pity, though. It would have been nice to catch up with him after all these years. Yes, it's been almost four years. Good Lord, so it has.'

'Uh, Paul, shall we get going?'
'Well, I'll tell you, John. I'm tired, I'm very, very tired. Frankly, the more I think of the work we have to do today, the less I feel up to it. I slept so badly last night. Naturally, you'll have noticed few of the usual telltale signs of fatigue. Bloodshot eyes, to take the

obvious example. But I rather feel I need to rest a little this morning. Rest and think. Do you mind?'

'Course not. Is there something I can do in the meantime?'

'Yes, there is. You can tell me about the Rembrandt. That's what I'll be thinking about. I can't just launch into the text without giving it some prior consideration.'

'All right.'

'Then, while I'm resting, maybe you'd like to have a go at the jigsaw puzzle? How does that sound?'

'Sounds good. Just as long as you won't expect me to have it finished by the time you're up and about again. It's a long time since I've done a jigsaw.'

'Jigsaw *puzzle*. The jigsaw is the actual saw that carves the pieces, you know.'

'Well no, I didn't.'

'No one does. Anyway, no, I won't expect you to have finished it. But the sooner you start, the sooner you will have.'

'That's right.'

'So. The Rembrandt?'

'Let me see, I jotted everything down. Here. Okay. Title: "Self-Portrait at the Age of –"'

'Sixty-three?'

'Correct. And it was painted in – ?'

'1669?'

'Correct again.'

'A few days before his death, am I right?'

'Ah no, sorry. Months. Four months.'

'Four months? Are you sure?'

'All this information I got from the plaque on the wall.'

'Four months? I was sure it was days.'

'No, months. Will I go on?'

'Please.'

'Well, you were right, of course. His nose is very bulbous. There's a funny little highlight right on its tip.'

'And, as I recall, a tuft of grey hair just under his lower lip.'

'No.'

'No?'

'He's badly shaven. There's bristle on the whole lower half of the face. But no, there's no single tuft of hair. Not the way I think you mean.'

'God, my memory. Go on.'

'His hands are splayed.'

'Splayed?'

'It's hard to say because the painting's so dark it's almost murky, but he seems to have his two palms outspread on his knees. One on each knee.'

'The hands aren't clasped?'

'No. Why, did you think they were?'

'Yes. Yes, I thought I did, but I – I just don't know any longer. He *is* looking straight into the spectator's eyes, I trust? A sad, serene, self-sufficient sort of gaze?'

'That's right. Quite hypnotic. You feel it would be indecent to get too close. Just as though he were a real person in front of you.'

'That's well put. Pity.'

'What?'

'Pity the eyes are precisely what's going to disappear when you do the jigsaw puzzle.'

'That's right.'

'Eyes, you know, John – the artist's eyes scrutinizing the subject's eyes, when artist and subject are one and the same – eyes are what self-portraiture is all about. You could paint a fine and moving and lifelike self-portrait that dispensed with every single facial feature *except* the eyes.'

'I'll go on, shall I? His hair, which is grey, billows out on either side of his head. He's wearing some sort of soft suede beret.'

'Thank Christ for that.'

'What do you mean? Why thank Christ?'

'Because that at least I *do* remember correctly.'

'You're smiling again, John. Please don't smile at me behind my back.'

'You really are good. I *did* smile, it's true. I smiled at

the idea of your thanking Christ he was wearing a suede beret. There was no malice in it.'

'I know. It's just me showing off. Let's see if I can identify the last piece of the puzzle myself. He's wearing a beige jacket, probably also suede, buttoned up in front. And it's got a fur-lined collar. Am I right or am I right?'

'Nearly.'

'Nearly?'

'The collar isn't fur-lined. It's of the same material as the jacket. And, yes, it does seem to be suede.'

'Oh God, oh dear God.'

'Why, what's the matter, Paul?'

'Can it be my memory I'm losing now?'

'Paul, they were just details. Trivial little errors. Nothing serious.'

'For me that fucking fur-lined collar *is* serious! It's deadly serious! If I can't even remember my own favourite painting!'

'You said yourself you hadn't seen it in years.'

'John, when I lost my sight, I lost the present. Utterly. All right. I've learned to live with that loss. Just about. But if I start to lose my memory, it means I'll lose the past as well as the present. Which leaves only the future. And, Jesus Christ, Jesus Christ, what a future!'

'I hadn't thought of it that way.'

'I've been living in a fool's paradise. A fool's hell, rather.'

'But, Paul, as long as I'm here, you haven't lost the present. Let me be your present from now on. *And your past.*'

'Now that sounds like a kind proposal, John, but since we both know you won't be here for ever, why bother making it at all? If there's one thing in this world I loathe, it's the sort of generosity that consists of extending offers both parties know will never be taken up.'

'Well, I'm sorry, I was only trying to –'

'I believe I'll go and lie down now.'

'Oh. Okay.'

'If you could have a look at the Rembrandt puzzle, I'd be very grateful.'

'Of course. And don't think too hard. Try and get some rest, too.'

'I'll see you later.'

∾

I know now I've taught myself nothing, memorized nothing. All those years and nothing to show for them. I'm helpless, helpless – and, save for John, completely alone in the world. Sightless, eyeless, faceless and alone, autistic, visually autistic, exiled from the humdrum vibrancy of the world. Oh, has anyone ever, ever been in such desperate

*straits? What is the world to me now but a blank sheet of
paper, a blank black sheet of paper from which every trace of
text is fading fast. What I would give – my right arm, my left
arm, my legs, my nose, my fingers, my cock, everything! –
for one more glimpse of that world!*

∾

'Well, make sure you dope him to the eyeballs. I rec-
ommend lots of Beechams and Lemsips.'

'They're good too. Make him sweat it out.'

'Uh huh.'

'No, no, not at all.'

'Don't you worry, it won't be a problem. I'm not a
half-bad cook, you know. I should be good. I've had to
fend for myself for long enough.'

'His little ways? Oh yes, I'm getting used to them.'

'Well, then. Why don't you just take the week off?'

'I mean it. In fact, I insist.'

'Don't worry. I'll speak to Sir Paul about it myself,

but I know he'll agree. And of course you'll get your pay in full, so don't let that worry you.'

'No, don't bother calling in. If there's anything I need, I'll ring you.'

'That's right.'

'That's – yeah, yeah, of course.'

'Good. Well –'

'Well, look after yourself. And be sure to give my very best to Joe.'

'Right. Bye.'

'Yeah.'

'I will. Well, bye now.'

'Bye.'

'Oh, Paul, it's you. I didn't notice you standing there.'
'I take it that was Mrs Kilbride you were talking to?'

'That's right. She rang to say that Joe was ill. He's come down with flu.'

'If I heard you right, you gave her the week off?'

'Well yes, I did. He seems to have it bad and –'

'That's all very well, John, but didn't it occur to you to consult me first? Before dispensing with her services?'

'Look, Paul, you told me – more than once you told me – not to stand on ceremony with Mrs Kilbride. That she's here for me just as much as for you. Isn't that what you said?'

'True. When it's a matter of making coffee or serving up the apple crumble. As for not coming in for a whole week, well, I'm still the one who pays her wages and – I'm not angry, mind you, I really am not, but I do feel I should be consulted on her comings and goings.'

'You were asleep. I didn't want to wake you.'

'I wasn't asleep. And couldn't it have waited till I was awake?'

'What are you saying? I was wrong to tell her not to come in?'

'Not wrong, exactly. I might well have told her the same thing. I just believe it *is* my job to tell her.'

'Sorry.'

'I'd certainly have made some sort of alternative arrangement before so cavalierly burning my boats.

Now what are we supposed to do about meals? Place an ad for a cook in the Post Office window, I suppose. God knows what that'll draw out of the woodwork.'

'I told you before I'd be delighted to cook for us both. This evening, if you like.'

'If I like? This evening it's got to be. If we're going to eat at all.'

'Listen, Paul. Why don't I do some shopping in Chipping Campden today and tonight I'll serve us up something a bit special. What do you say?'

'Well . . . well, all right, I don't deny a change from Mrs Kilbride's perennial stodge *would* be welcome. But will you be able, and willing, to cook every day for the next week?'

'I enjoy cooking for two. It's not a chore, it's a pleasure.'

'In that case, it's settled. All's well, etc. Have you had a look at the jigsaw puzzle?'

'Naturally.'

'Well?'

'Completed all the square bits. The outside edges.'

'You have? Why, that's wonderful, John. Half-way there, in my experience of jigsaws.'

'Puzzles.'

'What?'

'Jigsaw *puzzles*. Remember? The jigsaw is the saw?'

'Yes, John, in my experience, you're already half-way there. Just as with poetry. I don't suppose you knew I'd published a volume of poetry?'

'No, I didn't. I'm not much of a reader of poetry.'

'Juvenilia, just juvenilia. The slimmest of slim volumes.'

'Ah.'

'As Cyril Connolly almost said, inside every fatuous man there's a slim volume struggling to get out. Eh?'

'Sorry, I don't get it.'

'Oh, never mind, never mind. Lots do. Anyway, it was rhymed verse, pretty putrid stuff, I fear, I haven't looked at it in years. Thank God it died the death. There's no worse enemy of promise than success, as the same Cyril Connolly almost said. I do remember, though, that I invariably began with the rhymes just as you began the jigsaw puzzle with the straight edges. That was my point. It was nothing.'

'I'd like to read them. Your poems, I mean.'

'No, you wouldn't, and you won't. We've better things to do with your time. Like writing my book, for example. Shall we set to it? The morning's all but gone.'

❧

'I'm sweating again. How long have we been at it?'

'Let's see. It's nearly half-past five now and we

started at twelve, just as the church clock chimed. An hour off for lunch and half-an-hour, say, for coffee. That makes four hours in all.'

'Just four hours? Not enough, not nearly enough. Oh well. Read it back to me, will you. Then we'll unwind with a glass of whisky.'

'Read what we did today?'

'Just what we did today.'

'Are you sitting comfortably?'

'Just read it, please.'

'"Let us now consider the case of Rembrandt van Rijn. This man – this artist at the close of his earthly existence, old and unlovely, yet also serene and self-sufficient, whose last self-portrait hangs in the National Gallery, his two hands splayed upon his knees before him as if to say to the spectator, accept me as I am, as with age I have become – this man looks out at us from the canvas with the same two eyes with which he, the artist, looked at that same canvas three hundred years ago. He is only four months from his own death – or, should I say, from his immortality. His eyes, though, those eyes we feel it would be indecent to approach too closely, as indecent as though he were a real person in front of us, his eyes are what the painting is about, are what it is a painting *of*. For it is less a self-portrait than a study of eyes, a study of the eyes which saw first what we see now and which appear to gaze at us gazing at them, making eye contact with us across an abyss of three centuries.

'"With *us*, I say. But I, *I* have no eyes to gaze at Rembrandt's. I cannot make eye contact with him or with anyone in the world. And yet I do continue to 'see' those eyes of his even if I have been unable to see the portrait itself for several years. I see them with that so-called inner eye which has remained unscarred through all the trials and travails of my recent existence. Rembrandt's eyes have gone; and mine, too, have gone. Yet those four spectral eyes, his and mine, continue to make contact, his by virtue of representation, mine by virtue of memory.

'"Let us imagine, now, his 'Self-Portrait at the Age of 63' as a jigsaw puzzle on a tabletop. No, why imagine it? It exists. The National Gallery sells just such a puzzle in its souvenir shop. Imagine it, though, complete save for those few pieces, no more than three or four, that would fill in Rembrandt's eyes. What would we see? The landscape of a human head and torso. Or, rather, straight-edged and rectangular as it would be, the map of such a landscape, with, at its centre, a table-top-textured, jigsaw-shaped space, as amorphously curvate as a Hollywood star's swimming-pool, where the eyes would normally be."'

'Well? What are you waiting for?'

'That's it.'

'That's it? That's all we did?'

''Fraid so. It's not too bad, considering. I've just done a word count. Four hundred and seventeen.'

'Hmm.'

'We can always continue.'

'No. No, let that do for now. But I wonder. Does it actually mean anything?'

'In my opinion, it means quite a lot.'

'Thanks for the kind thought, John, but I can't help wondering if it's a load of guff. Now if I could only *see* it, I could judge it.'

'The painting?'

'The text!'

'Ah.'

'That business about the inner eye. The inner eye? What crap it is, really!'

'Oh well. Heigh-ho. Tomorrow's another day, as someone said.'

∾

'The plate's very hot.'

'Well, John, whatever this is, I can already tell it most certainly isn't *à la* dear old Ma Kilbride.'

'Pheasant at noon, sautéed potatoes at three, French beans at seven.'

'Mmm. How delicious it all smells. Even though "Pheasant at Noon" sounds like the title of some dreadful well-made play by Rattigan or N. C. Hunter. Is there bread sauce, by any chance?'

'Yes, indeed. Bread sauce at, let me see, I know you prefer me not to be too finicky about these things, but I'd have to say it's at about ten-past ten.'

'Ten-past ten, eh? You know what time that is?'

'Sorry? I'm filling your glass, by the way. Chambolle-Musigny 1990.'

'I beg your pardon?'

'The wine. You were saying?'

'Was I? What about?'

'Ten-past ten?'

'Oh yes. Yes, it's the time you'll always find on advertisements for wrist-watches. Always.'

'Really?'

'It has the effect of making the watch-face "smile", you see. Thereby rendering the watch more attractive to a potential purchaser. So the argument runs.'

'Really? However did you find that out?'

'Paul? Is there –'

'Is your notepad on the table?'

'Naturally. Why? Have you thought of something?'

'The watch-face. Ten-past ten. Like a blind man's face, don't you get it? What I told you before? About a blind man having to turn himself into the salt of the earth? Always smiling – always smiling – his face is always set at ten-past ten, just like a watch-face – making it easier for him to – to – ingratiate himself with those – with those acquaintances whose help he might have to rely on one day. Jot it down, will you.'

'Done.'

'Thanks. It's not bad, don't you think? And I fancy I know just where I can put it.'

'You're smiling, John.'

'Sorry, it was the way you said, "I fancy I know just where I can put it." It sounded almost ribald.'

'Yes, yes, I get that.'

'You really are amazing, though. You're like Sherlock Holmes. You catch me out every time.'

'Well, you know, John, I probably ought not to be divulging the tricks of my trade, but I have to tell you there's nothing supernatural about it. When you smile, you crease your lips and you smack your tongue – very faintly, very faintly, but you do – and you release a sort of funny nasal sigh. To a blind man it's all perfectly audible. I really can *hear* you smile.'

'Rather a scary thought.'

'That depends on why you're smiling, doesn't it? Now, I'm sorry, but I've been so very absorbed by this delirious chit-chat of ours you're going to have to tell me again what time it is on my plate.'

'Pheasant at noon. Potatoes at three. French beans at seven. And bread sauce at ten-past ten.'

'Thank you. Incidentally, that's quite an opulent aftershave.'

'*Jazz*. Saint-Laurent. Not too overpowering, I hope.'

'Not at all. Discreetly pungent is how I'd describe it. It might have overwhelmed one of Mrs Kilbride's insipid concoctions but this – well, my congratulations, John, this pheasant is delicious, yes, really very delicious.'

'My pleasure. Literally. It's been so long since I've cooked for two.'

'So you already said. But –'

'Yes?'

'Why, John?'

'Why what?'

'Why is it so long since you've cooked for two?'

'You know why. I live alone.'

'But that's what I mean. Why do you live alone?'

'You're still young. You appear to be relatively well-off. And you're clearly personable, more than personable. You told me yourself, on our first day together, that you'd admit to being good-looking. Now I don't wish to pry, but I can't deny I'm curious and you after

– 117 –

all have come to know rather a lot about me. So why is it you've never married?'

'I don't know the answer to that.'

'Don't you like women?'

'What?'

'Don't you like women?'

'Do you mean, am I queer?'

'"Gay" I think is the word nowadays. *Is* that what I meant? I imagine it was. You understand, it wouldn't make the slightest difference to our collaboration.'

'No, I'm not gay.'

'Then why is it you're alone? Forgive me, John, but you're living in my house and I know next to nothing about the existence you led before you came here and, freak I may be, but I'm no less inquisitive about my fellow creatures than any normally constituted human being.'

'Why don't we just say I've always been something of a loner.'

'Come now, John, that's not answering the question, merely prompting me to rephrase it. Why have you always been something of a loner? Tell me about yourself.'

'If you don't mind, Paul, I won't.'

'Ah.'

'After all, part of being a loner is that you don't want to talk about your life, right? I mean, think about it. If I really felt like opening up, then I wouldn't be the loner I am. You see what I'm getting at?'

'What I see is an ingeniously sophistical attempt to avoid the question altogether. So be it. If you'd prefer not to talk about yourself, then I respect your discretion. But if ever you do feel ready to open up, as you put it, please remember you have a friend here who'll be glad to listen to what you have to tell me.'

'That's kind of you, Paul.'

'Yes, John, this meal really is delicious. Or did I say that already? The pheasant is just right. Tender, not too stringy. And the potatoes – the potatoes simply melt in the mouth.'

'How do you find the bread sauce?'

'The bread sauce? Yes, it's also extremely nice. It has an odd, subtle sort of flavour. A flavour I can't quite put my finger on. Odd but, no, really, really very nice.'

∽

'Whoooo
    Let me know she's mine?
        Whoooo
    Made me feel so fine?
    Feel absolutely fabulous,
    Feel fabsolutely abulous!
        Whoooo

Da da da da dum?
        Whoooo
Da da dee dee dum
        Toooo?
Yes, you guessed it right!
No one but you.

        'Whoooo –'

'Who *is* that?'

'Is someone there?'

'John, is that you?'

'Say something, for Christ's sake!'

'John! John! John!'

'I'm here! What is it? Is something wrong?'
'Come inside quick!'
'You mean, inside the –'
'Yes, yes! Come right in! What does it matter?'

'What's happened?'
'Answer me honestly, John. Were you, just a minute
ago, were you standing inside this bathroom?'

'What? Of course I wasn't.'

'Look, I don't care why – whether you made a mistake – whether you imagined something or – I don't care. I just have to know if you were standing there. At the door.'

'No, Paul, I wasn't, I assure you.'

'Where were you?'

'When you called? I was sitting at the table, doing the jigsaw puzzle. I've almost finished it.'

'I suppose there's no point in asking you whether you saw anyone? I mean, in the hall or –'

'No, of course not. There's no one in the house but us. I locked the front door myself.'

'And the back door?'

'It hasn't been open all day. What happened? You thought someone was standing over you while you were in the bath, is that it?'

'I don't know, I just don't know any longer. The light *is* on, isn't it?'

'Yes, it's on. Paul, there's no one in the house. Take my word for it.'

'Yes. Yes, you're right of course. I got such a fright, though, you can't believe. My heart's still pounding. I really could have sworn –'

'Listen, I know you blind people become particularly sensitive to – well, that your other senses become hypertrophied – is that the word?'

'Yes.'

'Isn't it possible, then, you've become *too* sensitive? Isn't it possible you're beginning to hear things – things, creaks and the like, that are really nothing more than the ordinary wear-and-tear of an old house – and you end up making too much of them? Isn't that possible?'

'Yes, I – yes, I'm sure it is. Yes, you may be on to something there. Oh God, I'm in an awful state. How embarrassing for both of us. But, I tell you, John, I could have sworn, I could have *sworn*, there was someone else in the bathroom.'

'Would you like me to stay?'

'What? No, no, that's very kind of you, but I – I must be getting out anyway. The water's gone all tepid on me. Thank you, John. And apologies again that you've had to put up with such a silly billy. This can't be very pleasant for you. Above and beyond the call of duty, I'm afraid.'

'Don't think about it. What you need's a good night's sleep.'

'Yes, I do. I really do.'

∾

Am I imagining things? Am I? Could I have become over-sensitive, as John suggests? I never heard of that happening to a blind man, but it does make sense, it makes a lot of sense.

I hear a faint creak on the bathroom floor and I automatically assume it must have been 'caused' – caused by someone, that is. Yet, it's true, there do exist effects without causes. Things creak by themselves. They move of their own volition. Things happen, and there's no reason why they happen at one specific moment and not at another, not a minute before or thirty seconds later. Life is not a novel, it has no obligation to justify its every micro-event. Could it be, then, that merely the presence of another person in the house, after so many years of total solitude, has made me hypertrophically alert to the sounds and sensations that those who've always lived with others take for granted and end by hardly hearing at all? That would also make sense. I may simply have forgotten what 'company' sounds like. Or am I going mad? For madness would make sense too.

୬

'That you, John?'

'No, Sir Paul, it's me, it's Missus Kilbride.'

'Mrs Kilbride? What on earth are you doing here? You've got the week off.'

'Ah know, ah know. But ah forgot ma sewin in the kitchen – an ma *People's Friend* – an ah wantet to see fer maself everythin was runnin smoothlike. Thought ah'd pop over early, let maself in before eether a you boys got up.'

'Boys!'

– 123 –

'You know me. Ah just do it to tease.'

'Yes, well, don't. What time is it, anyway?'

'Just gone seven. Didnay ye hear the church clock go?'

'If I'd heard the clock, do you suppose I'd be asking you?'

'Ooooh, someone got out a bed the wrong side this mornin. What are you doin up so early anyways? Long as ah've known you, you liked a good long lie-in.'

'I had another bad night.'

'*Another* bad night? Not been sleepin properly?'

'No. Any coffee handy?'

'Ah only just put the kettle on. You poor dear, you dinnae look well and thassa fact. What you need is vit-amins.'

'Please, Mrs Kilbride. I'm not in the mood.'

'Just makin conversation.'

'That's exactly what I complain of. Why do people feel they have to talk all the time? Our mouths are also for eating but we don't eat all the time, do we?'

'Thass what you say. You'd change yer tune if ye saw ma Joe. Eat? ye'd think –'

'By the way, how is Joe?'

'Oh, Sir Paul, ah'm that worriet. Ah never seen him so peelly-wally.'

'Come, come, Mrs Kilbride, buck up.'

'Oh but, Sir Paul, if ye could only see him yerself, ye'd realize –'

'Now now. I'm sure there's absolutely nothing for you to concern yourself about. Just a bad bout of flu, isn't it? Uh, coffee ready?'

'Gie it time. Water's not boilin yet.'

'"No . . . No, the water's boiling . . ."'

'Whassat ye say?'

'Why, it's not boilin at all, Sir Paul. What are ye talkin about? Ye canna see it anyways.'

'Sorry, Mrs Kilbride, I was miles away.'

'Obviously. Like somethin hot fer breakfast? Scramblet eggs?'

'No thanks. Just toast.'

'No, Mrs Kilbride, I was thinking of a little boy I used to know. A long, long time ago. We were bathing together. The Suffolk coast. I should say, he was bathing. He'd already plunged in while I was still standing on the beach, gingerly dipping my toes in the sea. And when I asked him if the water wasn't freezing, he called out, "No, it's boiling! The water's boiling!" Wasn't that adorable? I called back, "If the water's boiling, why aren't there any bubbles?" But by then he was much too far out to hear me.'

'You bathin? Thass hard to believe.'

'I wasn't always the gargoyle you see now.'

'Wid ye like butter on yer toast?'

'Please.'

'Marmalade?'

'On the second slice, not the first. That is, if you're making two.'

'Ah am. John not up?'

'No. John's someone who also likes a long lie-in.'

'It's just that ah was pokin around next door and ah saw that jigsaw on the table all joint up.'

'It's finished, is it? Good, that means we can get started on it today.'

'It's got somethin to do with yer book, then?'

'Naturally it has. I got John to bring it back specially from London. From the National Gallery. Isn't the coffee ready yet?'

'Here. Here ye are. And here's yer toast. One on the left's the butteret one.'

'Thanks.'

'Whassit suppost to be?'

'What?'

'The jigsaw?'

'You're asking me that question? You've got eyes, haven't you?'

'Aye, but what ah mean is, whassat funny thing

between them?'

'Funny thing between your eyes? Venturing a wild guess, I'd say it was your nose.'

'Oh yes, ha ha ha, ah don't think. Ah mean, in the jigsaw. Funny thing in the jigsaw.'

'*What* funny thing?'

'On the floor. Lyin flat between the two a them. Ah triet lookin at it every which way, but ah canna make head or tail a it.'

'And I can't make head or tail of what it is you're saying. A piece of kitchen roll, please.'

'Here ye are. The thing – the – thass just it, ah dinnay know what it is. Kine a proppt up between the two men.'

'For God's sake, what two men?'

'The two men in the jigsaw.'

'What did you say?'

'Aw look, now you've droppt yer piece a toast. An naturally – sod's law – it's fallen marmalade-side down. Let me get a –'

'Oh, forget the bloody toast. What did you just say?'

'Well, you dinnay have to shout at me, Sir Paul. Ah know you didnay sleep very well, but ah'm still entit-let to some respect.'

'Please, please, Mrs Kilbride, this may be very important. What was it you said about the jigsaw?'

'Just that ah couldna work out what that thing was on the floor.'

'You said, between the *two* men, didn't you?'

'Aye, thass where it is.'

'But what two men? There's only one in the painting.'

'What paintin?'

'The jigsaw! It's a jigsaw of a famous painting!'

'Well, ah can tell ye there's definitely two men. And the thing.'

'Come into the living room with me.'

'What? This minute?'

'Yes, this minute. It's very, very important.'

'Aw Gawd, what've ah said now? Aw, all right. Hold on.'

'Please hurry.'

'Ah'm comin.'

'All right now. Tell me, is the box around?'

'The box? What box?'

'The jigsaw-puzzle box. I mean, the box the puzzle came in.'

'No . . . No, ah canna see such a thing. It's no on the table.'

'Okay, then. Okay. Look – just look at the puzzle itself and describe what you see.'

'Anythin to humour you. Well, there's these two men.'

'How are they dressed?'

'Like in olden times. One a them looks like Henry VIII, cept he's thinner. The other like he could be a minister. A priest more like.'

'And what's this thing you keep talking about? On the floor?'

'Well, thass it. Ah tell ye ah dinnay know. It disnay seem to be anythin really. Anythin ye can get a grip on. It looks all squasht and stretcht.'

'All squashed and stretched?'

'Tell me, Mrs Kilbride, could it possibly be a drawing of a skull?'

'A skull? No, never!'

'Are you positive? Look, put my finger on it!'

'Yer finger?'

'Yes! This finger!'

'Aye, okay. What ye say ye want me to do with it?'

'I want you to direct it down on to what you call the thing.'

'It's on it now.'

'Now look at it sideways. I don't mean my finger, I mean the thing. Look back at it from this direction.'

'Okay, okay, ye dinnae have to shove me.'

'Sorry. Just follow my finger back. Are you following it?'

'Ah am.'

'Now what do you say? Couldn't that represent a skull?'

'Well – well, yes, maybe. Ah suppose it could be a skull at that. But if it is, it's not what ah call well-paintet.'

'Never mind that. Now, just above the thing, is there a table?'

'Aye.'

'And on the table is there a lute?'

'A what?'

'A sort of mandolin. Like a guitar.'

'Thass right.'

'And a globe of the world?'

'Aye.'

'All right. One last question. If I'm not mistaken, the two men are standing in front of a curtain. Am I right?'

'Aye.'

'What colour is that curtain?'

'It's green.'

'Green, yes. Of course it's green. Thank you, Mrs Kilbride, thank you very much. I won't need you any longer. I've got the picture. Hah, yes, I've got the picture.'

❧

'Morning, Paul.'

'Ah, John, it's you. A very good morning to you. Sleep well?'

'Not bad. And you?'

'Me? Oh, fine. Just fine, fine.'

'I'm not used to finding you down here before me.'

'No?'

'Well, no. You been up long?'

'An hour or so. It was such a glorious morning I didn't feel like stopping in bed.'

'Glorious morning? Actually, it's overcast.'

'Well, it felt glorious to me. What's the difference if you're blind? I'm up. And, as they say, rarin' to go. R, a, r, i, n, apostrophe – rarin'.'

'I'll put the kettle on. You must be dying for your coffee.'

'Oh.'

'What's the matter, John?'

'There *is* a pot of coffee here.'

'Did *you* make it, Paul?'

'Me? Of course not. I'm utterly helpless, as you know. No, if you feel like thanking someone, thank Mrs Kilbride.'

'Mrs Kilbride?'

'Yes, Mrs Kilbride made the coffee. Have some.'

'So Mrs Kilbride's been here?'

'Uh huh. She forgot something. Her sewing basket, I seem to recall. I suspect she really wanted to snoop around the kitchen *and* the living room – to see what was what. In fact, she confessed as much.'

'She find anything not to her liking?'

'I really couldn't say. We just chatted about this and that. Aren't you having any coffee, then?'

'Yes, of course. It's just that –'

'Yes?'

'Paul, there's something on my mind.'

'Something on your mind?'

'Yes, I've been meaning – I've been meaning to –'

'If there's something on your mind, don't pick at it, man. We don't want it to scab.'

'I've come to know you quite well, Paul, and in a funny way being around you has meant that my own – my own sensitivities have been refined. Just like a blind man's. Just like yours, in fact. I'm starting to pick up – what is it you call them? – nuances? I'm starting to pick up nuances better and quicker than I used to. The tone of your voice, for example. I've become sensitive to the slightest shading in your voice. Your sarcasm can be pretty heavy, you know, and then other times it's really quite subtle. Yet I can instantly hear it in your voice and I can usually tell what's coming. It's like I've sprouted antennae, like I hear things I never heard before. I don't know if I'm making myself clear?'

'What you're saying makes perfect sense. Go on.'

'Well, this morning. This morning there's an edge to the tone of your voice which tells me something's definitely up.'

'Ah. Meaning?'

'Meaning? Meaning, I think, that you know something I don't.'

'I know lots of things you don't.'

'Putting two and two together, Paul, the tone of your voice combined with the fact that Mrs Kilbride was here, and we both know what a blabbermouth she can be, well, I may be sticking my neck out, but I'm willing to bet you – you already know about the jig-saw.'

'I do.'

'I was going to tell you, I really was.'

'Oh yes? What were you going to tell me, John? What possible excuse could you find for deceiving a blind man?'

'You have to believe me when I say –'

'Why should I believe you? Why should I believe anything you say? I'm disgusted with you, John, I'm truly, truly disgusted. I won't pretend I'm more hurt than angry, for I'm not. I'm very angry indeed.'

'You have every right to be.'

'Deceiving a blind man? I can't get over it. That's

evil, John, that's evil. How can you live with yourself?'

'I know.'

'Oh, you and yourself, you deserve one another!'

'If you'll only let me explain –'

'Explain? What can there possibly be to explain? What on earth did you hope to achieve by such pathetic chicanery?'

'Just let me speak, will you? When I was in the National Gallery, when I bought the jigsaw –'

'It's Holbein's "Ambassadors", right?'

'Mrs Kilbride told you?'

'Mrs Kilbride? She wouldn't know Holbein's "Ambassadors" from a turtle's turd.'

'So how did you find out?'

'I felt it with my sensitive little fingertips. A jigsaw puzzle is in braille, after all.'

'You did? Why, that's –'

'Oh, don't be such an ass! I figured it out for myself. That's all you need to know.'

'So, John? You were saying?'

'It's true, there *was* no Rembrandt jigsaw, just as you suspected there wouldn't be. But, and don't ask me why, I decided to buy the Holbein instead. It was purely on impulse, it was just a whim. At that moment, I swear, Paul, I *swear*, I had absolutely no intention of passing it off as the Rembrandt. It just seemed like – I don't know, it just seemed like a fun thing to buy. Then, when I got home, I mean when I got back here, and you asked about the trip, I don't know what came over me. You seemed so low, so depressed, I suddenly found myself telling you I'd managed to buy the right one after all. Paul, I only wanted to please you. Since you wouldn't be able to see it anyway, I didn't think it would make much difference one way or the other.'

'I see. It was just an impulse. Just a capricious whim. Yet you actually sat down and did the Holbein. You finished it. You chose to keep up the illusion. You even let me dictate to you a passage from my book about how such a jigsaw puzzle wouldn't have to be imagined because it really existed. Why, John? For Christ's sake, why?'

'God, I felt awful about that. I felt so awful – I felt so awful I was convinced you'd be able to hear the panic in my voice. I didn't know what to do. You must understand, I thought the jigsaw was to be just a – just a metaphor. I didn't realize you actually planned to write about it. I repeat, it was stupid thing to do, but it was to please you that I did it.'

'Well, John, I confess I no longer know what to think.'

'If you want me to leave, I'll understand. I'll pack

my bags and go right now if that's the way you want it to be.'

'It's the way it ought to be.'

'Then that's it? You want me to go?'

'Oh dear God, I wish I knew!'

'If you do go, it means you leave me here with what? With a handful of pages and an expensive, useless computer. On the other hand . . .'

'All right. All right. Now listen to me, John. I want you to listen very carefully to the question I'm about to ask you.'

'I'm listening.'

'Then this is the question. Can I trust you?'

'Paul, I –'

'I may be mad, I may be digging myself into a deeper hole than ever, but can I trust you never to play such a stupid trick on me again? Never to humiliate me as you've done?'

'I assure you, Paul, that wasn't at all my intention.'

'Answer the question. Can I trust you?'

'Yes.'

'Very well, John. I'm prepared to accept that what has happened was an aberration. End of story. We'll have no more apologies, no more excuses. We'll never speak of it again.'

'You mean you'd like me to stay?'

'It's certainly what I seem to be saying.'

'I really appreciate that, Paul.'

'And, John?'

'Yes?'

'Get rid of the Holbein. Not just off the table but out of my house.'

'I'll do it at once.'

'One last thing.'

'Yes?'

'I just made some remarks to you that weren't very pleasant.'

'Paul, I deserved them. You needn't apologize.'

'I know you deserved them and I haven't the slightest intention of apologizing. It wasn't at all what I was going to do.'

'Sorry.'

'And I've told you before, stop saying sorry all the time. I don't like it.'

'It's just a tic. I'll try to curb it.'

'What I was going to say was that I made some extremely unpleasant remarks and one of them was something about "How can you live with yourself?" Do you remember?'

'Yes, of course.'

'And then, you may also remember, I added, "You and yourself, you deserve one another!"'

'Yes.'

'Note it down, will you.'

'Right.'

～

'Brrr. It's chillier than I thought.'

'Maybe if you knotted up your scarf?'

'Maybe you're right. Hold on a second.'

'Yes, that's much cosier. Well, John, shall we take the opposite direction tonight?'

'What, and walk out of the village altogether?'

'No. Not if we turn right at the corner and go round the village counter-clockwise instead of clockwise.'

'Okay.'

'You know, Paul, when you speak of going round the village counter-clockwise, you make it sound a bit like the clock method. Church at eleven, pub at three, herd of sheep at nine.'

'Sheep? Are there sheep out at this hour?'

'Well, yes, yes. They're grazing on the field beyond the common.'

'Goodness. What time *is* it?'

'It's earlier than usual for us, don't forget. Just after seven.'

'Even so. What about the common itself?'

'Kerb. What about it?'

'No children playing on the swings, I suppose?'

'Actually, there are. Three.'

'Can you make them out?'

'Just about. Up on the kerb.'

'Describe them to me.'

'There are two young girls on the roundabout. Twelve-year-olds, maybe thirteen. They may even be twins. They've both got on what look like navy blue overcoats, though I could be wrong about the colour, it's already dark. Anyway, they've both got overcoats and scarves and they're both wearing what I think you call bobble hats.'

'I don't seem to hear any girlish screams or giggles.'

'They're just silently spinning around.'

'And the other, the third child?'

'That's a little boy, I think. Hard to tell from here. He can't be more than five or six.'

'Disgraceful. He ought to be in bed. Probably got oafish parents just out of their teens. Couldn't care less what their offspring get up to. They should be made to pass a test before being allowed to reproduce. What's he doing?'

'Standing there. Watching the two girls. He's a forlorn little creature.'

'I bet he is. How's he dressed? Snugly wrapped up, I trust?'

'Appears to be. He's got a bobble hat as well.'

'And mittens? Is he wearing mittens?'

'Mittens? Oh, I can't possibly tell from here. Kerb.'

'Pity. I have a great fondness for children's mittens.'

'Really?'

'Mmm.'

'May I ask why?'

'I adore those little mittens that toddlers have. You know, the kind that are attached to their coat sleeves by a cord and dangle from their little wrists as they waddle about. Why I adore them I couldn't really say. I just do.'

'Yes, I suppose they're quite cute. I mean – sorry.'

'Why sorry?'

'Because I bet you hate that word "cute".'

'No. No, I've nothing against it. Why should I?'

'No reason. Just thought you might. Shall we walk through the churchyard? It's still open. Or else go straight on?'

'Straight on, I think. Leave the dead in peace. Why don't you describe the effect of the church steeple against the sky?'

'Well, it's very English. What you might call quietly dramatic. The steeple itself, as I'm sure you're perfectly well aware, is oblong and rather chunky. Not pointed. Not the soaring type that seems to sway against the sky as you watch it. It's got its two feet on the ground, it's got no – it's got no – no Gothic pretensions.'

'No aspirations to the sublime.'

'Exactly. And it doesn't pretend to have. And the sky itself is English somehow. It isn't lurid, it isn't spectacular. Yet I still find it affecting in its modest way.'

'Colour?'

'The sky?'

'Yes.'

'Dark grey. Bluish-grey. Almost metallic. The clouds – there's a bank of them hovering over the church – the clouds are drifting but very, very slowly. Trying to catch them at it would be like trying to catch a clock hand moving.'

'Nicely put. You know, John, you may well end up becoming a writer yourself one of these days.'

'Coming from you, that's a serious compliment.'

'I mean it. You have a real eye, a real visual imagination. Indeed, you've got too much imagination. *Viz*, as they say, *viz* the jigsaw puzzle.'

'Look, Paul, I'd like nothing better than to apologize all over again for what I did. In fact, it's actually frustrating for me not to be able to keep on telling you again and again just how sorry I am – kerb – to keep on telling you just how sorry I am till I'm blue in the face from apologizing and you're blue in the face from listening to me. But you did insist the subject was to be a closed book, so I'm just going to have to hold it in.'

'What did you say?'
'I said I'll just have to hold it in.'
'No, no, no, before that?'
'Before?'
'Your exact words!'
'I said the subject was a closed book.'
'A closed book! Magnificent! That's it!'
'That's what?'
'A closed book, don't you see? A closed book!'
'I'm sorry?'
'Capital A, capital C, capital B. A Closed Book. The perfect title for *my* book!'
'You mean instead of *Truth and Consequences*?'
'Oh, I never did like that title! *Truth and Consequences*! So pompous! No, no, *A Closed Book* is ideal. It'll look wonderful on the cover. Just imagine it in Dillons or Waterstone's. *A Closed Book*! Just think of it. Who, now who, browsing in Waterstone's and catching sight of a book with that title, could ever resist opening it?'
'Yes, I see what you mean.'
'Jot it down, will you, jot it down. Not that I'm likely to forget.'
'Right.'

'*A Closed Book* . . . You know, John, I have you to thank for that. I know we've sworn not to talk about you-know-what but this, I must tell you, more than makes up for it.'

'You really feel that strongly?'

'I love it. In fact – Oh! Christ! Ow!'

'Oh shit, Paul, that was my fault. I'm terribly sorry. I was so busy thinking about – well, I forgot all about the kerb. You all right?'

'Well . . .'

'No, seriously, I –'

'Not to worry, not to worry. A blind man must learn to take the odd bump and bruise in his stride.'

'I'm *really* sorry.'

'Frankly, I'm so euphoric I barely felt it. Alighting on the right title for a book is one of the very few privileged moments in a writer's wretched existence. Well worth a stumble or two.'

'It's amazing. I've never seen you so happy.'

'You can't deny it's been a remarkable day. It began so catastrophically, didn't it? Yet, workwise, as the Americans say, workwise it's turned out to be deeply satisfying. How many words did we get down on paper?'

'On the screen? Fifteen hundred and something, wasn't it?'

'Our best yet. Then there were those delicious lamb

cutlets you made for supper. And now this. *A Closed Book*. When you think about it, it's almost symbolic.'

'How do you mean?'

'Why, don't you see? Apart from giving me the perfect title for my book, the phrase can also be applied to the unfortunate little incident of the jigsaw puzzle.'

'Yes, Paul. Except, don't forget, that's precisely how it came up.'

'Hmm?'

'If you remember, it was when I was apologizing for the jigsaw incident that I used the phrase in the first place.'

'Now now, John, don't go spoiling things.'

&

'It's a heavenly day today, today!
What a heavenly day today!
It's a heavenly day for makin' –
Hey!
What do you say?
Goin' my way?
Wanna make hay?
On this heavenly day, today, today,
This heavenly day today!'

&

A heavenly day? What, rather, a strange day it's been. And what a strange person John is. And what a strange person I am, for that matter. Blindness, though, does make strange bedfellows. If anyone had told me I'd offer house room to an individual who had actually had the gall, the vicious gall, to take advantage of my blindness, I would have called him a cretin. And yet there he is, a man who committed an offence akin to stealing sweets from a baby, there he is, asleep in the room next to mine. No matter that he was responsible for giving me my marvellous title, I cannot forget that John also did that. But why? Why? Could he really have been trying to please? It's possible, yes. Yet any intelligent person would have realized, would have known from a kind of intimate conviction, that it was absolutely the wrong thing to do, that it was the act of a moral philistine. It's true, to be sure, that we all of us commit acts we know to be stupid and callous and wrong-headed, we know to be all of that even as we commit them. It's what is called human nature. To err is human. And John too is human.

∾

'What on earth is that racket?'

'John!'

'Sorry? Oh, it's you, Paul. Sorry, what?'
'Can you please turn that off, whatever it is.'
'Oh. Right.'

'There. Sorry about that.'

'Thank heaven! Where was it coming from?'

'My radio. I have a little portable radio. Didn't I mention it to you?'

'No, you didn't.'

'Oh well, yes, I have.'

'Did it have to be so excruciatingly loud?'

'I'm sorry. I thought you were in the bathroom. I didn't think I'd be disturbing you.'

'I took my bath last night. So what was it?'

'The music?'

'Yes, John, the music.'

'The Who.'

'The what?'

'Not the What, the Who. They're a rock group. Sort of *passé* now, I guess, but –'

'I know who the Who are. I'm not a dinosaur, you know. For your information, Freddie Ashton once commissioned me to write the argument, as it's called – with, I assure you, very good reason – the argument of a ballet to music by Pete Townshend. Wasn't he one of the Who?'

'Yeah, he was. And did you?'

'I did. It was called *Rigmarole*.'

'*Rigmarole*? Afraid I've never heard of it.'

'Not many people have.'

'A flop?'

'A hideous flop. As it deserved to be, I may say, with its cacophony of a score. Still, I did get to meet Townshend, which was a mildly vertiginous experience for both of us.'

'You two hit it off?'

'Our encounter was, let us say, a semi-success. He hung on my every *other* word.'

'This time, John, I fear I cannot hear you smile. Perhaps it's because you feel I might have said that before?'

'No, no. I was just thinking of you and Pete Townshend together. You have to admit it's a bit of a mind-blower.'

'Would you like to paw the hem of my dressing-gown?'

'Well, no, thanks all the same, Paul. I'm not *that* much of an admirer. Impressed none the less. Coffee?'

'Please.'

'You must have been quite upset to hear of his death.'

'Whose death?'

'Pete Townshend's, of course.'

'Pete Townshend? Pete Townshend is dead?'

'Why, yes. Why, Paul, I'm sorry. You didn't know, did you?'

'Well, obviously I didn't. Pete Townshend dead? Poor fellow, what did he die of?'

'He was assassinated.'

'Assassinated? You mean *murdered*?'

'Sorry, of course I mean murdered. I'm sorry, Paul, I'm being – it just seems so strange that you – but of course you couldn't be expected to have heard about it. It happened, oh, two years ago, a bit more than two years ago. He was gunned down by a fan. Well, by some young druggie who claimed to be a fan. Outside the Groucho Club. It made front pages all over the world.'

'Yes, well, I never do see front pages, as you know. Or any other pages, for that matter.'

'But, you know, John, what with . . . I mean to say, I'm really starting to think that maybe I should.'

'Should what?'

'Pay more attention to what's going on.'

'I'd be happy to read the newspaper to you if you like.'

'Yes, that's an idea . . . Yes, that might be . . . Pete Townshend dead . . . In a funny way I'm rather sorry to hear that. Not that I . . . Not that I ever knew him well or ever . . . Yes, maybe you *could* start to read the news headlines to me. One isn't a saint, after all, one isn't a monk. Blind as one is, one does continue to live in the world. I say, John, you wouldn't have a newspaper here, by any chance?'

'Actually, I do. I got one in the village this morning when I went to buy the milk.'

'Which is it?'

'The *Guardian*.'

'The *Guardian*? Oh well, never mind. Read from it anyway, will you? Just skim the essential information off the top.'

'Now?'

'Why not?'

'All right. Here's your coffee.'

'Thanks.'

'Want anything to eat with that?'

'No thank you. Just some headlines.'

'Okay, let's see what we've got here. The prime minister has just arrived in Havana. First time a British premier has visited Cuba since Castro assumed power. Questioned about the trip, Mr Cook sought to make it clear that –'

'Mr *who*?'

'Cook.'

'Let me get this straight. What's his name? His first name? Roger, isn't it?'

'Whose?'

'Cook! Cook!'

'Robin.'

'Robin Cook! And Robin Cook is prime minister?'

'Yes, of course he is.'

'But – but what about Blair? Don't tell me he's dead too?'

'Blair resigned.'

'*Resigned*? You're saying Blair *resigned*? Already? When? And why? What's going on, John? What in heaven's name is happening to the world?'

'Things change, Paul. Things change.'

'Never mind the philosophy. Just tell me why Blair resigned.'

'Well, they tried to keep it a secret, but there are some secrets that simply can't be kept. He has AIDS.'

'AIDS? Tony Blair?'

'Afraid so. It got into one of the tabloids. The *Mirror*, I think. Then, naturally, all the other newspapers were obliged to pick it up. Why, were you an admirer of his?'

'Don't be grotesque. It's just that – good grief, man, don't you see? I never knew! I never knew! And now that I do know, I don't just feel blind, I feel so very *stupid*. And I refuse, I categorically *refuse*, to believe that a blind man has to be stupid.'

'Well, I don't –'

'Oh, just go on, will you.'

'There's been a terrible massacre in Northern Ireland.'

'Nothing new there. I'd have been surprised if you'd said there hadn't been a terrible massacre in Northern Ireland.'

'The Reverend Ian Paisley was one of the victims.'

'And they say there's no such thing as good news. Go on.'

'Bill Gates has announced he's a born-again Christian. He's decided to bequeath his entire fortune to charity.'

'Never heard of him. Go on.'

'O. J. Simpson has committed suicide.'

'Good riddance. Go on.'

'Madonna is set to marry the actor Michelangelo DiCaprio.'

'Heard of her, never heard of him. Go on.'

'Princess Diana has been sighted in Bhutan.'

'What?'

'Princess Diana has been sighted in Bhutan.'

'You're pulling my leg.'

'No, really. It says here that a group of American tourists claim to have seen Diana on a knoll.'

'On a what?'

'A knoll.'

'What's an oll?'

'A knoll? A little grassy hill?'

'Oh, a knoll! You must learn to pronounce it correctly. Knoll.'

'Knoll.'

'Go on.'

'Well, they claim they saw her standing on a – on a knoll in Bhutan holding her two arms out in front of her in a beseeching manner. Then she seemed to fade away. Anyway, that's what it says.'

'What tripe. What absolute fucking garbage. If that's what the world has become – and I don't mean Diana, I don't only mean Diana, I mean what the *Guardian* deems fit to plaster over its front page – if that's how things have changed, then I can only say I'm well out of it.'

'You want me to continue?'

'No thank you.'

'Ah? Now I wonder who that can be?'

'I'll get it.'

'Could you?'

'Hello?'

'Oh, hello. Long time no see. Paul, it's Mrs Kilbride.'

'Oh, not too badly, considering.'

'Uh huh.'

'As it happens, we have. If I say so myself.'

'No, I've been doing all the cooking.'
'John, tell her we've been eating *extremely* well. Tell her you've turned out to be quite the little chef.'
'Sir Paul wants me to tell you we've been eating *extremely* well. That I've turned out –'

'No, of course not. He was only teasing.'

'Yes, he was!'

'Come on, Mrs Kilbride. What's happened to that famous Glaswegian humour of yours?'

'Yes, I have.'

'Yeah, that too. But what about you? When are we going to have you back here?'

'Oh.'

'Oh, I see. When did you –'

'No, no, of course not. How is he?'

'I wouldn't dream of it, Mrs Kilbride. No, you've got to be at Joe's side. But I'm sure it'll turn out to be a false alarm.'

'True. As you say, even so.'

'Absolutely. And –'

'I realize that, Mrs Kilbride. And I'm not going to tell you not to worry, because I know you're going to anyway. But until he's had the tests the very worst thing you can do is start imagining things.'

'Well, yes, but –'

'Uh huh.'

'Yeah.'

'Look. No, just – no, no, listen to me.'

'Listen to me. I'm sure Sir Paul agrees with me that you've got to stay with Joe as long as you have to. He's actually nodding at me as I speak.'

'Tell her that if there's anything I can do for them, either of them, just to let me know. Anything at all they might need. Money, anything.'

'You hear that, Mrs Kilbride?'

'Of course, of course, he just meant that –'

'Yeah. Whatever.'

'Okay, yes. And –'

'And give Joe my very best.'
'From me, too, John.'
'That was Sir Paul again. He wants you to give Joe his best too.'

'All right.'

'All right.'

'Bye.'

'Yeah, well, bye now. We'll speak. Bye.'

'Bye.'

'Good grief, John, what a woman! Why is it impossible to get some people off the phone?'
'She sounds terribly worried.'
'Did I understand correctly? Joe is seriously ill?'

'He seems to have some kind of pneumonia. He's been told he has to have tests.'

'Ouch. The dread word.'

'She's afraid it might be cancer. Lung cancer.'

'Lung cancer. Oh God. Joe's been a three-packet-a-day man for as long as I've known him.'

'For the moment I suspect it's all in her head. What it means, though, is that we're going to be on our own a bit longer than expected.'

'Hmm. Think you'll be able to cope with the cooking? Or shall I try to arrange for someone else to come in? Though heaven knows who.'

'Of course I'll be able to cope. I really do enjoy cooking for two. And it hasn't interfered with our work so far, has it?'

'No, to be honest, it hasn't at all. Pity, though. In a way, I'll miss Mrs Kilbride. Most of the time she sets my teeth on edge. Yet I do rather enjoy having the old bag around the house. Heaven only knows what would become of me if you weren't here.'

'But I am here, Paul.'

'That's right. You are.'

'And unless you'd like another cup of coffee –'

'No thanks. No, it's time for work. All going well, we ought to be able to finish what we're doing by the morning's end.'

'So you said yesterday.'

'Hmm, yes.'

'A penny for your thoughts, Paul.'

'What sort of day is it today?'

'What sort of weather, you mean?'

'Yes. It feels sunny.'

'It is. It's a beautiful day. There's a real sense of spring in the air. When I went into the village this morning, I noticed little clumps of crocuses and daffodils on the common. You feel the new year is finally getting its act together. Why do you ask?'

'Ask what?'

'About the weather.'

'Ah, well, you see, John, if we do manage to finish by midday, then rather than launch into a whole new section I might ask you to make one of your little excursions.'

'To London?'

'No, no. To Oxford.'

'Oxford?'

'Yes, I'd like you to drive over to Oxford and do another little recce for me. It's less than an hour from here. Take your camera. And the notebook, of course.'

'Any particular area of Oxford?'

'Well, of course a particular area. I'm not writing a travel guide, you know. I want you to visit my old college. Hertford. I need a good, detailed description of the building and its grounds.'

'So you're finally going to deal with the past?'

'Mmm.'

'What about the period of your life before and after Oxford?'

'What about it?'

'Do you also plan to write about your childhood? Your adolescence? Oh, and weren't you once briefly a schoolmaster?'

'Who told you that?'

'What?'

'That I was a schoolmaster?'

'Well. No one, really.'

'No one told you? It's just one of those facts of life you didn't have to be told?'

'Honestly, I can't remember where –'

'Can you see me as a schoolmaster?'

'Oh, I don't know. I seem to remember having schoolmasters who weren't unlike you.'

'Is that meant to be a compliment?'

'Frankly, Paul, I didn't mean much of anything by it. Is something the matter?'

'Let's just drop the subject, shall we? As for my early life, I told you before that mine is not destined to be a conventional autobiography. On the rare occasions, on the very rare occasions, that I read autobiographies, I always skip the earliest years – the author's childhood, his family tree. Who cares? Every childhood is more or less alike. If I'm reading the book at all, it's because I'm interested in the subject when he *ceases* to be a child, when he's already become the sort of person who deserves a biography in the first place. Anyway, that's the way *I* feel. And since I do feel that way, I certainly have no intention of forcing my own childhood down the reader's throat. All right?'

'Yes, Paul, that's clear enough. When do you want me to start?'

'When we've finished what we still have to do. Or after lunch. Whichever comes first.'

'Right.'

'Oh, and John, see if you can put your hands on some little guide-book to Oxford's gargoyles.'

'Sorry?'

'There are lots and lots of gargoyles in Oxford. On the college roofs, mostly. And since you obviously won't be able to get a good look at them yourself, you'll have to buy a guide-book. Every newsagent sells them.'

'Oh, I see.'

'Do you mind?'

'Not in the least. It's what I'm here for. Besides, I haven't been to Oxford for ages.'

'Neither have I.'

❧

He's gone. This needs some serious thought. But what precisely am I to think? Have I gone blind not only literally but figuratively? Am I becoming, as I feared I was becoming, stupid? Or is it perhaps the case that what John suggested is true? Accustomed to solitude as I am, accustomed to living in my own imaginative world (like an artist, indeed!), is it that I've started to see – to hear, to sense, whatever the appropriate verb might be – the latently abnormal in every manifestation of the overtly normal? When one comes down to it, the latent is all I know. If I no longer possess the humdrum human capacity to combine, harmoniously combine, the latent with the overt, the unfamiliar with the taken-for-granted, it's because, unlike those with eyes, there is absolutely nothing now that I can permit myself to take for granted. With John's presence, though, the overt, the taken-for-granted, has once more entered my life, and the balance is as yet so unequal everything suddenly feels askew, awry. John sits there calmly at the breakfast table, my breakfast table, describing a world to me which bears as little resemblance to the world I know as – yes! – as Holbein's 'The Ambassadors' does to a Rembrandt self-portrait. The world I know, I say. But, after four years of no contact whatever with that world, four years of no newspapers, no wireless, no television and, above all, no interest, who knows what has hap-

pened to it in the meantime? I can't help thinking of that whiskery old music-hall joke about British xenophobia – 'Fog inChannel. Continent isolated'. Fog in my vision – to put it mildly. World isolated. Except that it's you yourself who're isolated, arsehole! You! You! You! It's you who've changed. The world described by John has changed less, far, far less, than you have. Oh, why did I allow myself to become such a recluse? Why didn't I – 'Now who on earth is that?'

'Yes?'
  'Hello?'

  'I say, hello? Is someone there?'
  'Well, of course someone's here. Who are you?'
  'I'm from –'
  'Hold on, hold, will you. I'll get the door.'

  'Yes, yes? Who is it?'

  'Ah. I, uh . . . As I say, I'm from . . . uh . . .'
  'Speak up. Never seen a blind man before?'
  'Oh yes, I – that's to say, I assure you, it was just –'
  'For goodness sake, what is it? What do you want of me?'
  'Oh, well, I'm from your local Conservative Party Association. As you know – uh, as you probably know – we have elections – the local elections? – coming up

in a few days – and I was, I was, well, wondering, you know, I was wondering whether we could count on your support?'

'You mean you got me up from –'

'Yes, I'm – I'm tremendously sorry to have disturbed you. I – I didn't realize – well, thank you so much for your time.'

'Wait.'

'What?'

'Wait there. Yes. Why, yes, there *is* something you can do for me. Look, why don't you come in?'

'No, no, really, I can't. Thank you for – but, you do appreciate, I have several other –'

'I'm not an ogre, I'm not going to eat you. Come in. It'll only take a minute.'

'No, really no, I should be –'

'What are you saying? You can't spare five minutes to be of service to a blind man?'

'Ah. Well, I –'

'Has the Conservative Party become so smug, so ungracious, so bereft of compassion, it can't even take the time to help out one of its less fortunate constituents?'

'Well, uh, yes, when you put it like that. Yes, of course I must –'

'Good. Then come in. We shall both catch cold chattering on the doorstep.'

'Thank you. But only for a few minutes, you understand.'

'Yes, yes, I know. Close the door behind you, if you don't mind.'

'In here.'

'Ah, yes. Yes, indeed. This is, uh . . .'

'It's where I work. It's called a study.'

'Aha. So this is where you work?'

'With my amanuensis.'

'With your . . .'

'Now listen. At that Conservative Association of yours?'

'Yes?'

'There are computers, right?'

'Uh, yes, of course. We're completely –'

'Good. Ah, but wait, are they Big Macs?'

'Are they what?'

'Big Macs. Is it Big Macs you use or – Oh, bloody hell, I don't remember the name of the other sort.'

'I'm afraid I don't know what you mean. Big Macs are –'

'Look. Look at this computer here.'

'I'm looking.'

'Recognize it?'

'Of course, it's a – it's a Mac.'

'Well, for God's sake, why have we been talking at cross purposes? So you do know it?'

'Uh huh.'

'Know how to use it?'

'Yes. That's to say, I think so. It isn't quite the same model –'

'But you can use it?'

'Yes, yes, I can. What exactly is it you want of me?'

'What I want of you – you know, you really ought to consult a doctor about that snorting of yours. It can't be healthy to snort as much as you do.'

'Well now, look here, I –'

'Sorry, sorry. A blind man is all ears, you know, all ears. But to come back to the computer, what I want you to do is switch it on.'

'Switch it on? Just switch it on?'

'Yes, just switch it on. I cannot myself, you understand. If you could do it for me, you'd be doing me a very great favour.'

'You want it switched on now?'

'Yes please.'

'Well, uh, let's see here. I presume it's all plugged in at the back. Yes, yes, seems to be. Well, it should switch on just here. Like so.'

'There it is.'

'Ah yes. How well I know those chimes.'

'Now, unless I'm mistaken, it'll take a few seconds for it to light up.'

'That's right. It's just coming up now.'

'Good, good.'

'Well, Mr, uh – if that's all you – I'll – I'll be –'

'No, no, stay. There's something more I need from you.'

'Excuse me, you're hurting me.'

'Am I? I'm sorry. But listen. Sit down here, will you?'

'Now really, I just don't have the –'

'Nonsense. I said it would be a matter of minutes and it will be.'

'Well...'

'Please just sit down.'

'Oh well, all right.'

'Good. Now tell me what you see.'

'On the screen?'

'On the screen.'

'Well, for the moment not much. Just the usual icons. Hard disk. Anarchie. Documents. Launcher. Java. And the wastebasket, of course.'

'What in heaven's name is all that?'

'They're applications. They come with the computer. Would you like me to open up the hard disk?'

'Is that what you're supposed to do?'

'Look, I've done it already. Now I can see the list of folders and documents. Not that there are many. This computer hasn't been used much, has it?'

'Hasn't it? It certainly feels as though it has.'

'Well, there's next to –'

'No, no, when I think of it, I suppose it hasn't. Tell me, do you see something called *A Closed Book*?'

'A what?'

'*A Closed Book*. Is there some – some folder or document titled *A Closed Book*?'

'No. Nothing like that.'

'Nothing at all? Are you sure?'

'Quite sure.'

'There must be. Take another look.'

'I'm telling you, no. There's just the one folder. It's called *Truth*.'

'*Truth*? Why, of course, yes, that would be it. Silly of me. John forgot to rename it.'

'What?'

'Never mind. Can you open it?'

'Well, if you –'

'Indulge me, please.'

'It's open.'

'Okay. Now read it.'

'What? All of it?'

'Just the first paragraph. Please.'

'"I am blind. I have no sight. Equally I have no eyes. I am thus a" – uh –'

'Go on, go on.'

'"I am thus a freak. For blindness is freakish, is – is – surreal. Even more surreal than my blindness itself, however, is the fact that, having been dispossessed not only of my sight but my eyes –"'

'"But *of* my eyes –"'

'"But *of* my eyes, I continue to 'see' nevertheless. What it is that I see may be 'nothing' – I am blind, after all – but that 'nothing' is, paradoxically, by no means beyond my powers of description. I see nothing, yet, amazingly, I am able to describe that nothing."'

'That's enough. Yes, that's fine, that's fine.'

'Ah. Now, uh, I can't say how glad I've been to have – to have been –'

'Bear with me for a few seconds more. Seconds, I do assure you, not even minutes.'

'Well, all right, but –'

'Just go to the end, will you?'

'The end? The end of what?'

'The last part of the file. You can do that, can't you?'

'Ohhhh. Yes, I suppose I can. Let me – okay, I'm there. What now?'

'Read to me again. Just start at some suitable place and read on. Please.'

'Well then . . . I'll begin here, shall I? Um . . . "Para-doxically, perhaps, the question I have asked myself of *Sitting at the Feet of Ghosts* is not why it enjoyed the (for me) unparalleled commercial and critical success which it did – to be candid, I always knew that it was destined to please – but, rather, why I should have elected to write it at all. So utterly dissimilar to my other novels it is –"'

'"*Is it –*"'

'"So utterly dissimilar to my other novels *is it*, so superficially stylish and glamorous – I think of the period setting, of Venice, of the predominantly aristo-cratic milieu – that even now I have difficulty recog-nizing it as one of my own. Was it – by 'it', I mean my original motivation – was it merely that, having been for so long described as a writer's writer, I craved just once in my career to be regarded as a reader's writer? Hardly. I claim neither knowledge nor understanding of the great invisible constituency of my readers." Is that enough?'

'No, no, not yet. Go on, please.'

'"Or else did I hope to catch the collective eye of the theretofore indifferent critical fraternity? Again, hardly. It is, as I already knew, impossible to prejudge a critic's judgement unless –"'

'Sorry, would you mind? "Prejudge" and "judge-ment" within the space of just two words. How could I

have let that pass? Change "prejudge" to "predict",
will you? No, wait. Change it to "anticipate". Yes,
"anticipate". Do that now, will you?'

'Really, I haven't –'

'Just do it. It won't take a second.'

'I've done it.'

'Go on.'

'"It is, as I already knew, impossible to anticipate a
critic's judgement unless one happens to be cognizant
of his tastes; and, in my experience, what the majority
of critics like best is money. Or, finally, did I simply
prefer to be a – a – a – whore than an old maid? In short,
had I brazenly decided to, as they say, sell out? A third
time, hardly. The writer who sells out always gets the
better of the bargain, since his public is bound to feel
short-changed and the work itself, in consequence,
will not, cannot, endure. But I should doubtless not
even try to comprehend my own novel's phenomenal
popularity. How, after all, can I judge a work in which
I myself am directly implicated? It would be exactly
like the police force choosing to investigate its own
corruption." That's where it comes to an end.'

'Thanks. Well, it all seems to be in order. Unless I've
misremembered, it's word for word as I dictated it.'

'Sorry, what?'

'Nothing. Just a little nagging anxiety. Foolish,

really. Yes, thank you again. You read that very nicely.'

'Well, thank *you*. Now can I go? I mean, would you mind if I went on my way? I really do have lots of other constituents to call on.'

'Naturally you can go on your way.'

'Thank you. By the way, you are a Conservative, aren't you?'

'Me? I've never voted in my life.'

'Well, really, I do think you might have –'

'Come, come, my friend. You've just set a poor old blind man's mind at rest. You've done your good deed for the day.'

'We're not the Boy Scouts, you know. But – yes, I'm – I *am* pleased to have been of assistance. So I'll just –'

'Switch the thing off before you go, there's a good fellow.'

'It's off now. So. I can't depend on your vote, I suppose?'

'Absolutely not. This way, this way.'

'I remember. Please, you're digging into my arm again. Do you mind?'

'Just making sure you don't lose your way. Through here.'

'Yes, yes, I know. Ow! I said, do you mind?'

'Sorry, sorry. Oh, and incidentally, while I'm at it, it *is* Cook, isn't it? I mean, the prime minister?'

'Cook?'

'Roger Cook.'

'Roger Cook?'

'That's what I said. Roger Cook.'

'Chap on television, you mean?'

'Well, I'm scarcely likely to know that, am I? With these? Take a good look.'

'Ohhhh, I –'

'See what I mean? But he is the prime minister, isn't he?'

'What? What? Yes, oh yes, whatever – whatever you say!'

'And Blair has AIDS?'

'Oh, absolutely! Absolutely! Blair has AIDS all right! Yes, it's – ah, thank heaven, here's the door. I mean – No, no, don't bother, I'll see myself out. I'm awfully glad – as I said before, awfully glad – to have been able to assist you. And, uh – well, I – well, good-bye.'

'Goodbye, goodbye. Drop in again some day.'

'Moron.'

∾

The computer didn't lie to me. Roger Cook is prime minister. And, it appears, poor Tony Blair does have AIDS. Everything is in order, is it not? And yet. And yet. Why am I unable to rid myself of the feeling that something neverthe-less is amiss? Is my mind at rest? No. Will it ever again be at rest? I wonder.

~

'Christ! Shit!'

'What the fuck was that?'

'A book? It's a fucking book. I could have killed myself! Who the fuck was stupid enough to leave a book on the landing? An open book! At the top of the bloody stairs!'

'Yes, who?'

~

'That you?'
'Yeah! Be with you in a minute! Just let me hang my coat up!'

'Well, hello there.'
'You're home sooner than I expected.'
'Traffic was light. Only thing that was, though. I've had a day-and-a-half, I can tell you.'
'Why don't you pour yourself a whisky? Unwind. You might get one for me, too.'

'Good. I need it.'

'You all right, Paul?'

'Mustn't grumble.'

'Ah. If I know you, that means you feel very much in the mood to grumble.'

'Does it? I'm not like that, am I?'

'Oh yes you are. So tell me. What's there been to grumble about?'

'Come on, Paul. We both know you're going to tell me eventually. Why not get it over with? What have I done now?'

'I nearly fell downstairs.'

'What?'

'There was a book on the floor at the top of the stairs. This book.'

'Ah.'

'What book is it?'

'Here's your whisky.'

'Thank you.'

'It's mine. *How Proust Can Change Your Life*. Alain de Botton. I've been reading it on my own time. I didn't think you'd object.'

'Well, of course I don't object. I do object, however, to falling downstairs. And please don't bother reminding me I didn't actually fall. No thanks to you I didn't. How Proust can change your life, eh? *You* almost changed my life.'

'I'm really sorry, Paul. I left it there because I meant to take it to Oxford with me. I leave books and other things on the stairs all the time at home. But of course it was stupid, and dangerous, to do it here. Really, I apologize.'

'Well – well, no harm done, I suppose. Chin chin.'

'Chin chin.'

'So? Find what you were looking for in Oxford? What *I* was looking for in Oxford?'

'I think so. I went to Hertford, as you asked, and I took lots of photographs, *and* lots of notes, just to be sure.'

'Did you go inside the college itself?'

'I tried to, but I was stopped by some officious, bloody-minded porter. I wondered if I ought to tell him what I was there for – who I was there for – but then it struck me you'd probably prefer I didn't.'

'You're right. I would. None of his fucking business.'

'It wouldn't have had any effect anyway. There were tourists milling about, mostly Japanese, some kind of coach party, and they were all being turfed out.'

'You photographed the bridge, I presume?'

'Naturally.'

'Isn't there a shield, some sort of shield, some sort of coat-of-arms, in the middle?'

'Uh huh. It's all in the camera.'

'Describe it for me.'

'Just let me get my notes.'

'It was hard to get a proper view of it with all the scaffolding and tarpaulin – they seem to be renovating the college.'

'Why can't they leave the bloody thing alone? There's a mania in this country for wrapping up public buildings. Last time I saw London, it looked like one of those ghastly conceptual experiments by – what the hell's his name – Hungarian or Bulgarian sculpture fellow – always wrapping things up? What *is* his name?'

'Christo?'

'Christo, yes. Very good, John, very good.'

'Thank you – *he answered wryly*.'

'Stop it. It's only me. You ought to be used to me by now.'

'I am. Oh, I am.'

'Yes, well, you don't have to agree with such gusto. Go on.'

'Go on?'

'Hertford. The coat-of-arms.'

'There are two stags, two stags' heads borne up to

heaven by cherubs, and there's also a – is it a fleur-de-lis? – on a zigzagging background.'

'Yes. Yes, that *is* how I remember it. Go on.'

'Well, the quad itself is rectangular, it's almost square, and the grass is very well tended. None of it has any particular architectural interest as far as I could see, except maybe for the ivied walls. There's a fountain – and – and what else? Yes, the stairs into the college are on the right as you pass through the entryway.'

'On the right? You're quite sure they're on the right?'

'Yes, I – wait. No, wait. I made a rough little map of the layout. No, I'm wrong. They're on the left. I was looking at it the wrong way up. They're on the left as you enter.'

'That's true, yes, they *are* on the left! Oh, John, to you this couldn't be more trivial, but to me it's extremely important. It's important for me to know that, about some things at least, my poor old memory hasn't failed me.'

'Well, it does seem to be okay as far as your Oxford days are concerned.'

'Yes, it does, doesn't it? But then, it should be. I was there for four years. And – and wait. Next door?'

'Next door?'

'Next door to the college, just beyond the bridge, there's a house, isn't there? There's a quaint little house with a brass plaque. Someone lived there, someone famous. Oh God, I used to pass that house every day of my life. It was a scientist, a – a – a – Edmond Halley! Edmond Halley lived there! You know, the boffin who discovered Halley's Comet?'

'Well, didn't he?'

'He may have discovered Halley's Comet but, no, he didn't live next door to Hertford College. The plaque's there all right, but it's for James Watt. Inventor of the steam engine?'

'James Watt? But Watt was a Scot!'

'So?'

'I mean, are you absolutely sure it was Scott?'

'Scott?'

'What?'

'You mean Watt?'

'Watt, yes, Watt! Are you sure it was Watt?'

'I took a photograph of the plaque.'

'Well, bully for you, John. You must show it to me when it's developed.'

'Look, I'm sorry, Paul, but I can only – I can only report back –'

'Yes, yes, yes!'

'I mean, look, it's –'

'Oh, never mind. The gargoyles, what about the gargoyles?'

'Ah, yes, I did manage to buy a guide-book. Surprisingly expensive.'

'Don't worry. I'll reimburse you.'

'Yes, Paul, I know you will. You really didn't have to say that.'

'Oh, sorry. I'm sorry. I'm – anyway, what is this book?'

'*Oxford's Gargoyles and Grotesques. A Guided Tour.*'

'*Oxford's Gargoyles and Grotesques.* Well, that's admirably pithy and to the point. What are they like?'

'Well –'

'What I mean is, do any of them bear the slightest resemblance to me?'

'Ah, so that's why –'

'Naturally. Why else?'

'Well? *Do* any of them look like me?'

'Remember, John, it's for the book. This is no time to be fastidious.'

'Frankly, and just riffling through it, I have to say it's a bit disappointing.'

'Disappointing? Why so?'

'Because they're not all that grotesque.'

'Not all that grotesque, eh? So none of them actually does look like me? As you say, that *is* disappointing.'

'Here's one from, let's see, the Bodleian Library.

"This sprightly gentleman" – this is the guide-book talking – "this sprightly gentleman – a stone spirit, or lapid –" Do you know what a lapid is?'

'Who cares? Go on.'

'"A stone spirit, or lapid one might call him – seems to be emerging from the wall."'

'Well, there you are. That's most promising. Could be me emerging from the mangled car in Sri Lanka.'

'Well, no.'

'Why not?'

'He's grinning.'

'I see. Try again.'

'Here's one from Brasenose. "A friar leans down from a window jamb and idly picks his nose."'

'No thanks.'

'This is an odd one. From Magdalen.'

'Pronounced "Magdalen".'

'"Magdalen." All it says is, "This monster beggars interpretation."'

'Sounds like Michael Jackson.'

'You've *heard* of Michael Jackson?'

'Of course I have. Who hasn't?'

'True. You never met him, I suppose?'

'No, I didn't. Let's stick to what we're about, shall we? What do you think? Could this particular gargoyle be useful for the book? Top me up, will you.'

'Oh. Right.'

'Here.'

'Thanks. About the gargoyle?'

'Well, Paul, I don't know whether you'll be pleased or not, but in my opinion it bears absolutely no resemblance to you.'

'Pity. And, I suppose, phew. Go on.'

'This next one's from Magdalen as well. And, since you keep insisting, I suppose I would have to say there's a faint likeness this time. If you half-close your eyes.'

'Yes, all right. What exactly is it?'

'It's a – well, no, simpler if I just read you the caption. "Man-monster and alligator are locked in symbiotic conflict, each grasping the other's tongue."'

'Intriguing. You wouldn't be trying to tell me something, John, would you?'

'Why? What do you mean?'

'If you don't get it, it's not worth explaining. Go on.'

'Come on, that's not –'

'I said, go on.'

'That's about all there is. Oh, no, here's something at New College. Now this could be interesting. A set of seven gargoyles representing the Seven Virtues. Patience, Generosity, Charity –'

'Forget it. Doesn't New College also have gargoyles of the Seven Deadly Sins?'

'Yeah, they're spread out on the next page.'

'Any of them remind you of you-know-who?'

'Well . . . At a pinch, number five.'

'Number five?'

'Sorry. That's the reference number. Number five is, let's see, "Corrupt Love".'

'I'm weary of this little game. Weary, period.'

'Oh. All right. You don't feel like taking a walk this evening, then?'

'Yes I do. Yes, let's. I need air. I've been trapped inside my head all day. You can't know how claustrophobic it is never to be able to escape from the inside of your own head. Yes, let's have our walk now. Early. While it's still light.'

∿

A man may be riddled by invisible superstitions. It's possible, for example, to imagine just such a man, one who, painfully conscious of how foolish he must appear to others when sidestepping each and every ladder propped up in the street, succeeds in persuading himself one fine day that walking under a ladder will bring good luck rather than bad and that not walking under a ladder will bring bad luck rather than good. From which moment on he will sashay along the street, nonchalantly walking under every ladder he encounters. And those passers-by who chance to notice him – and who no doubt say to themselves, Now there goes someone completely free of superstition – utterly fail to understand that he nevertheless is still in thrall, neurotically in thrall, to a wholly personal form of superstition, one which, for all that its effects remain invisible to them, is no less irrational and inhibitive than that of which it constitutes the negative image. I've become such a man. It's almost as though the daily routine of my life with John – coming up for a month now! – were ruled by an invisible set of precepts and principles that I'm helpless to resist. It's almost as though I've been led along the edge, the very rim, of an abyss, without realizing for an instant that what has accompanied me all the way is a precipitous plunge into the void.

∾

'Paul, what *is* that?'

'What is what?'

'On your forehead?'

'It's nothing.'

'Nothing? It's quite a bruise you have there. Here's your toast, by the way.'

'Thank you.'

'Butter to the left. Butter and marmalade to the right.'

'Thanks.'

'So?'

'So what?'

'What happened to you? The bruise?'

'Oh, that. It was the wardrobe door again.'

'What about the wardrobe door?'

'There's something the matter with the latch and the door doesn't always stay closed. Sometimes, not often but sometimes, it swings open by itself. I've got no way of knowing, so naturally I walk straight into it.'

'And you walked into it this morning?'

'Yes, I did.'

'I see . . .'

'It's happened before and it'll happen again. I've learned to live with it. A little more sugar, please. These days I seem to prefer my coffee sugary.'

'There you are.'

'Thanks.'

'How often has it happened?'

'Oh, half-a-dozen times, I suppose.'

'*Half-a-dozen times?* You're mad.'

'What did you say?'

'I said I think you're mad not to have had something done about it.'

'The blind must expect to be knocked about a bit.'

'Not when it can so easily be avoided.'

'Charles tried to fix it once and only made it worse.'

'Well, I've no idea what Charles did, but I know I can fix it.'

'Stop fussing, will you? It's not serious. I'll just have to be extra careful.'

'For a week or two. Then you'll forget again.'

'Well, and so what? It's my forehead.'

'Look, Paul. I'm going to be driving over to Chipping Campden after lunch. You've got practically nothing in the fridge for the weekend. And, as I remember, there's a locksmith in the High Street. So why don't I pop upstairs, measure the wardrobe door, then buy one of those things – restrictors, I think you call them. Door restrictors. They're like a pair of huge metal compasses. Like protractors. Remember? At school? Anyway, you screw them on to the door and it always swings shut. And stays shut.'

'I'd rather you didn't.'

'Why not? They're not expensive.'

'You know perfectly well I'm not thinking of the expense.'

'Well, what? It would take me twenty minutes to fix it. Top whack.'

'I said no.'

'This has nothing to do with your claustrophobia, has it?'

'Why do you say that?'

'That wardrobe of yours? It's very roomy. I was just wondering if you were afraid of getting stuck inside.'

'John. As someone once said, read my lips. I don't

want the lock changed and that's that.'

'Just a thought.'

'Let's get to work, shall we.'

~

'Read it back to me. I promise not to interrupt.'

'All right. I'm starting. "I myself heard of the Princess of Wales's death in a way likely to have been repeated up and down the country. On the Sunday morning in question, early, very early – I had only just emerged from my bath – a friend rang me up. His voice sounded bizarrely guttural.

'"'Well,' he said, without any of the expected tele-phonic pleasantries and preliminaries, 'and what do you think of the news?'

'"'News? What news?'

'"'You mean you haven't heard?' he exclaimed with feigned incredulity. (I say 'feigned', because, consid-ering my 'What news?', he could hardly have been in doubt that I had not heard.)

'"'The news burst forth in a loud firework display of exclamation marks.

'"'Diana's dead! Dodi Fayed's dead! They were being pursued by paparazzi! Their limousine crashed in a tunnel in Paris! The paparazzi have been arrested!'

'"'Like the entire country, I was caught off guard.

What was shocking was less the mere fact of Diana's death than how utterly out of the blue it had come. Even so early, however, I was already conscious of a faintly jarring note. My acquaintance was genuinely distraught: as I was later to learn, he would spend the remainder of that same Sunday in front of his television set. During his initial phone call, nevertheless, I could detect in his voice what I can only call a *terrible elation*, the elation of someone who knows himself to be the bearer not simply of bad news but of *thrillingly* bad news. He was aghast, but he was also audibly exhilarated. And, no matter that he himself would indignantly deny such an allegation, I am convinced that he would have been obscurely frustrated, even downright disappointed, had I replied to his opening question by murmuring, 'Yes, it *is* dreadful, isn't it?'

'"Everyone knows what I mean: the hair-raising excitement that we feel when communicating, to someone who has not yet been apprised of it, devastatingly bad news about mutual friends, colleagues and, of course, household-name celebrities. It is a species of excitement which has nothing to do with *schadenfreude*, the perverse satisfaction we (some of us) take in the reversals suffered by our friends. It can perfectly well coexist with authentic grief. But if anything can be securely filed away under the rubric of 'human nature', it is surely that half-suppressed frisson experienced when we find ourselves in a position to impart information – information that, like paint, is still wet – relating to an acquaintance's sacking, divorce, accident, arrest, suicide or terminal cancer.

'"To my knowledge, there is not, although there ought to be, a word for such a frisson, especially now that it has definitively gravitated on to the stage of world affairs. For take the case, precisely, of Diana. Whatever else there was to be said about it, the international response to the circumstances of her fatal accident was a vindication of McLuhan's theory of the contemporary world as a global village, one in which, by virtue of the ubiquitous electronic media, anything that happens somewhere will happen everywhere else as well at the same time. And just as a real village would be abuzz with the sudden, violent death of its most glamorous and stylish inhabitant, so the global village seemed to be engulfed by the – dare I call it 'gleeful'? – frenzy which surrounded Diana's.

'"It is not as though any of us wished for that death. Even I, profoundly hostile as I am to the brainless culture of celebrity, found myself saddened that someone so young and beautiful – someone, moreover, who appeared truly not to wish to fritter her life away – had met with so horrible an end. But there is no getting away from it. Diana's death, tragic, pointless, ironic or (grisly word) iconic, call it whatever you will, was also a phenomenon. It was tremendously *interesting*.

'"Nor was it unique, being, rather, only one in a lengthy series of recent newsworthy disasters which have had the effect of shaking a sluggish world out of a torpor of eternal sameness. For many of us, Pete Townshend was no more than a name, an irrelevant one at that, until he was slain in a Soho street. The Reverend Ian Paisley no more than an obnoxiously foul-mouthed (*sic*!) demagogue until he, too, was gunned down in his turn. Tony Blair no more than a toothily vacuous nonentity until he was enhaloed by the venomous spectre of AIDS. As for O. J. Simpson, there was, worldwide, an explosion of outrage at his acquittal, but there was equally (who will deny it?) a wonderfully galvanizing undercurrent of *relish* in that outrage, a relish of which the world would have been deprived if he had been sent to prison. The subsequent fact that he committed suicide was hence doubly gratifying, for it not only eliminated what vestiges of resentment might have lingered on from the patent – indeed, flagrant – injustice of his trial, it also offered yet another sensational item of news in which the collective, ever anxious to escape the cyclical ruts and routines of its humdrum, single-channelled existence, could revel without either guilt or responsibility.

'"What does it mean, though, to become oneself, as I modestly and briefly became, the focus, the cynosure, of such attention? What does it mean to become oneself the sensation, oneself the ten days' wonder? I have sometimes pondered on the perceptional abyss that separates the nervous flier – as he sits with fastened seat-belt and scrotum-tightening rigidity inside an aircraft – from some idly ambling pedestrian far below on the ground who, for no particular reason, happens to glance up at the sky and observes a minuscule, streamlined object gracefully traversing it. And I have wondered, too, whether death might not be a little like that. For the individual who is experiencing death, the individual *to whom it is happening*, it must feel like being *inside* a plane, inside a vast, hollowed-out metal cylinder. For the attendant observer, by contrast, it must feel like being *outside* a plane, watching it pass overhead, so far, so very far overhead, and so tiny, so very tiny, it becomes virtually impossible for him to imagine that there might be anyone inside it. There, perhaps, is the difference between death as perceived by a dying man and death as perceived by another who watches him die. And there, too, perhaps, is the difference between being, and merely revelling in, a sensational news item."'

'That's it?'
'That's it.'
'How many words? I'd say a thousand. No, twelve hundred.'

'One thousand and ninety-two.'

'Not bad, not bad. For a morning's work, that's not bad at all. Repetition of "ten days' wonder" and "I have wondered", but we can fix that. What do you think?'

'I think it's good.'

'You think it's good?'

'Uh huh.'

'Why, then, do I seem to detect a ghostly question-mark loitering with intent, as a policeman would say, at the end of that sentence?'

'No. I really do think it's good. Very good.'

'Come on, John.'

'What?'

'What do you actually think?'

'Oh well, if you insist. It just struck me as, well, as being more – I'm not quite sure how to put this – more . . . more journalistic, somehow, than the rest of the book so far.'

'Your point being?'

'I couldn't help wondering if . . .'

'Out with it.'

'Well, I couldn't help wondering – I mean, while you were dictating – I couldn't help wondering if you'd decided after all to recycle the article we talked about, remember? The article you wrote for the *Sunday Times*? The article about Diana? Adapted here and there, you know, to fit the new context, but basically the same. Am I right?'

'No. What's for lunch?'

∽

Why is it I'm glad, why is it I'm relieved, that John is out? What is it about him that makes me eternally ill-at-ease? Oh, God, for an old friend. Oh, for not necessarily a close friend but an old one. Someone for whom I haven't always been blind and disfigured.

∽

'Let me see – where – here it is. Now. Now this shouldn't be too difficult. Let's – oh damn, of course, they've changed over to these bloody – what are they called again? – what? what? what? what are they called? – oh shit, trying to find a word on the tip of your tongue, it's like – it's like a – it's like waiting for a sneeze to break. What *are* the fuckers called? Ah, ah – wait – touch-tone! Touch-tone phones. Yes, touch-tone . . . Dialling used to be so easy and so – so specific to phoning. But, no, naturally, naturally, they can't leave anything alone, they've got to fiddle with everything, even with the few things that miraculously do work. Oh well, let's go. Andrew's number, Andrew's number, Andrew's number. Oh no, I don't believe it! Come on. Remember, remember! What a time to forget!

Ohhhh, wait, wait, 631 something. Uh, 631 – 631 – 631.3341! 631.3341! All right now, don't forget. 631.3341. Now, let's see, here's 1, and here's – here's 3 – so this must be 6. Okay, that's good for 631. Now – 3341 – all right, all right now – 3 is here – and again – and 4 is on the other side – as so – right – right – and then 1 is directly above 4. Okay, right. Let's have a dry run. 6 – 3 – 1 – ohhhhh, no, that's 4 – no, no, it *is* 1, it *is* 1 – do it again. 6 – 3 – 1, right. Shit, what comes after 1? 6 – 3 – 1 – 3 – 3 – 4 – 1. So. 3 – 3 – 4 – 1. 3, 3, 4, 1. 3, 3, 4, 1. Okay. Now – go! 6 – 3 – 3 – damn, stop! All right, calm, calm, just keep calm – *and* – 6 – 3 – 1 – uh – 3 – and the second 3 – 4 – 1. *Et voilà.* Nothing to it.'

'The number you have dialled has not been recognized. Please check and try again.'
'What?'
'The number you have dialled has not been –'
'All right, all right. Okay, let's just check this again. 6, yes – 3, yes – 1, yes – 3, yes – 3 again, yes – 4 – 1. That seems all right. So. 6 – 3 – 1 – 3 – 3 – 4 – 1.'

'The number you have dialled has not been recognized. Please –'
'Stupid cunt! *Why* hasn't it been recognized? Don't you even know your own numbers? 631.3341. So what the hell's the matter with that?'

'Uh oh. London. London, of course. It's 0171! 0171.631.3341! Now. Oh God, now where the fuck's the 7? Wait. 1 – 2 – 3 – new line – 4 – 5 – 6 – then 7. Two rows directly under 1. Right. 0 – 1 – 7 – 1 – 6 – 3 – 1 – 3 – 3 – 4 – 1. Here goes nothing. 0 – 1 – 7 – 1 – eh, eh – 6 – 3 – 1 – 3 – 3 – 4 – 1.'

'Ah, at last.'
'Please hold the line while we try to connect you. The number you are calling knows you are waiting.'
'Now what?'
'Please hold the line while we try to connect you. The number you are calling knows you are waiting.'
'Yes, darling, I heard you the first time.'

'Wait, wait. I think – yes, I think I know what this is. It's – it's the – it's the – the call-waiting thingamabob. Call-waiting facility. Yup. Another useless gadget. Why *do* they do it? And what would happen, I wonder, what would happen if I dialled my own number? What? Let's see. I'd get the message first. "Please hold the line while we try to connect you. The number you are calling knows you are waiting." Then – then, yes, as the person being phoned, I'd find myself cutting in. Then what? Would I be put through to myself? Hah?'

'Wait, though, wait. Damn. I should have held the line and someone would eventually have answered it. That's what you're supposed to do, isn't it? Hold the line? Start again. 6 – 3 – 1 – no, no, damn it – start again – 0 – 1 – 7 – 1 – 6 – 3 – 1 – 3 – 3 – 4 – 1.'

'Please hold the line while we try to connect you. The number you are calling knows you are waiting.'
'Uh huh.'
'Please hold the line while we try to connect you. The number you are calling –'
'Hello?'
'I want to speak to Andrew Boles.'
'Sorry? Andrew who?'
'Andrew Boles.'
'I'm sorry, there's no one of –'
'Don't be silly. He's only the senior agent, you know.'
'No, he isn't.'
'Yes indeed he is.'
'I say he isn't. And I'll tell you why. Because this is a private number. And you – whoever you are – you're an asshole.'

'Oh God. What have I ever done to deserve this?'

'Could I have got the number wrong? 631.3341. 631.3341.'

'No! 631. 4 – 3 – 3 – 1. 631.4 – 3 – 3 – 1. Now, now I've got it. 631.4331. Oh God, after all this, Andrew, after all this, you'd bloody better be in. Here we go. 0 – 1 – 7 – 1 – 6 – 3 – 1 – hold it, hold it – 4 – 3 – 3 – 1.'

'Hello. Boles and Whitmore here. How can I be of help?'
'Ah. Yes, I'd like to speak to Andrew Boles, please.'
'Putting you through.'

'Hello. Mr Boles's secretary speaking.'
'Give me Andrew, please.'
'What is the matter regarding?'
'It's personal. Just put me through.'
'I'm sorry, but I'm afraid I'll have to –'
'I tell you it's a personal matter. Don't worry. Andrew will want to speak to me.'
'Nevertheless. Before I can disturb Mr Boles, I've got –'
'I'm telling you for the very last time. Andrew will want to take the call. Just do as you're told and stop fucking around.'

'Who shall I say is calling?'
'Ohhhhh. Look, tell him it's a face from his past. No, no, wait. Tell him – tell him – it's a ghost at whose feet he once sat.'

'Hold the line. I'll see if he can take the call.'

'Paul? Paul? Can that really be you?'

'Hello, Andrew.'

'Good Lord, it *is* you! Paul, how *are* you?'

'Oh well. I am what I am, you know.'

'Paul, this is terrific! I can't believe it's really you on the other end of the line! My God, I mean, after all these years!'

'Four years, Andrew.'

'Four years. Hmm. That *is* a long time, that's a very long time. And you haven't changed an iota, you old devil! At least, your telephone manner hasn't changed. You'll be pleased to know, I'm sure, that I have one very distressed secretary here. I can't imagine what you said to her. Or should I say, I can well imagine. Devil, you!'

'I assure you I was no more than my sweet reasonable self.'

'I'll bet. Oh, anyhow, what does that matter? What matters is that here you are, after all these years, on the phone just as though – I can't get over it!'

'It *has* been a long time, Andrew. Longer, I suspect, for me than for you.'

'Probably so, probably so. But, you know, Paul, I did try to ring you. I mean, I hope you know that. That I tried several times to ring you. Just after the –'

'I do know, Andrew, and – Well, let's just say that, even though I refused to speak to you, I was very touched by the fact that you'd called. In fact, I'd have been extremely hurt if you hadn't. It's just that back then, as you can imagine –'

'Yeah. Yeah, I *can* imagine, old chap. And, well, I'm not going to bring it up now because I'm sure it's the very last thing you'll want to talk about. But I'd just like you to know that I – well, what can I say? I've thought a lot about you these last four years. Jane, too, I know.'

'Thank you, Andrew, I appreciate that.'

'Sorry. Can you hold on a sec, Paul?'

'Yes, yes, I know. Oh, look, get his number and tell him I'll call him back as soon as I'm free. Oh, and Daria, hold all my calls, will you? Sorry, Paul, where were we?'

'Paul?'

'I was telling you how much I appreciated your not having forgotten me.'

'Well, of course, it's perfectly true. And what I'd really love now is to see you. Of course – of course I don't know how *you'd* feel about that?'

'I'm going to surprise you, Andrew, and say I'd love

to see you too. Yes. I do think maybe one day soon we might get together, just the two of us. Don't misunderstand me. I'm not suggesting you fix up a date now, so don't bother riffling through your – your –'

'My Filofax?'

'When I'm ready, I'll give you a call. If I may.'

'If you may? You must! You must! I absolutely insist on it, chum! Jane, too. I know Jane's dying to see you again.'

'Well, Andrew, she may think she is. But I'm not a pretty sight, you know.'

'You never were, old boy. Look, Paul, I respect what you're saying to me. I understand, I do. You must take your own good time and when you're ready – I mean, when you're ready to start seeing a few of your old, close friends again – well, you know what I mean – just pick up the phone. By the way –'

'Yes?'

'Just now? You did pick up the phone yourself, did you? I mean, it *was* you who made the call, was it?'

'Yes, it was. After several false starts.'

'Why, Paul, that's wonderful! That's really wonderful! And it's just the beginning, you'll see! There's no knowing what you're going to be able to do when you put your mind to it!'

'Maybe. Don't forget, though, that eyelessness is

what you might call an incurable disease. I mean to say, there's always going to be a ceiling on anything I achieve.'

'A higher ceiling than you may think now, old boy.'

'Maybe, maybe. Anyway, Andrew, I truly did need those dreadful years of solitude. I had to get them behind me before I could even contemplate doing anything new with my life.'

'I know, I know.'

'It's a bit like winning a set in tennis. All the effort you put into winning the set – then you finally do win it – and you wipe the slate clean and – I don't mean this in a pejorative sense – but then you can start all over again from square one. You follow me?'

'Of course I do, Paul. And I'm delighted that the – that the period of adjustment seems to be coming to an end. To be blunt, Paul, it's true I don't know what you look like, but you certainly sound as though you're back on form.'

'Thanks. And I'd like to thank you, too, Andrew, for not patronizing me. Even though I couldn't help noticing that the strain of *not* patronizing me, the strain of being so frank and all, so deliberately brutal, was just, shall I say, was just a wee bit audible, just a teensy bit self-conscious, no? Even so, I'm touched, I'm very touched.'

'God, no one can ever get anything past you. Still as

sensitive as ever to nuances, I see. Isn't that how you once defined a writer? As an entomologist of nuances?'

'Once? Many times, Andrew, many times.'

'Which brings us neatly to – dare I ask?'

'What?'

'No chance of a new book in the pipeline, I suppose?'

'Well, Andrew, since you do dare ask, the answer is yes.'

'Yes? Why, that's absolutely wonderful, Paul! That's wonderful news! I can't tell you how happy I am! And how excited! Happy for you and excited for myself!'

'It *is* rather exciting, isn't it?'

'And how! But what are we talking about precisely? What stage is it at? Is it still just a project? Still just a twinkle in . . . well, in . . .'

'Awkward, isn't it, Andrew?'

'Anyway, no. It's already considerably more than just a twinkle.'

'God, how exciting this is! A novel, I assume?'

'No. No, in fact it isn't a novel.'

'No?'

'I suppose we're going to have to call it an autobiographical memoir.'

'Better still! Better still! You know, Paul, even years

ago when – you remember, I tried to persuade you to write your autobiography?'

'Yes, except –'

'I tell you I just can't believe what I'm hearing. Has it got a title yet?'

'*A Closed Book*.'

'Sorry, what?'

'*A Closed Book*. The title's going to be *A Closed Book*.'

'Oh, Paul . . .'

'Why, don't you like it?'

'Don't I like it? I *love* it! I. Love. It. *A Closed Book*, it's genius! And listen – listen, Paul – you know, I think I can already begin to see the cover. Just listen. Tell me what you think. A closed book – I mean, the jacket illustration would be a picture of a closed book – and on the jacket of that book – I mean the book on the cover – there would be an illustration of another closed book – a smaller book, naturally – and then, on the cover of the smaller book, yet another closed book – and so forth. *Ad infinitum*!'

'Only potentially, Andrew.'

'Potentially?'

'Only potentially *ad infinitum*.'

'Pedant! You always were a pedant!'

'And proud to be one.'

'But don't you think that would make a wonderful cover?'

'Well, let's not get carried away. There's so much more to be written than already has been written.'

'Already has been written?'

'Why, yes.'

'You've already started the thing?'

'Yes, of course.'

'Paul, I'm hurt.'

'Oh, come on.'

'No, really, Paul, I'm hurt.'

'What on earth are you talking about?'

'Why is it only now I'm hearing about this wonderful new masterwork?'

'Come, come, Andrew, own up. You know quite well you're interested in my books only when they're finished. When there's money to be made out of them.'

'A lie, a barefaced lie. I'm interested in everything you do, whether it's likely to make me money or not. Just so happens it always does.'

'Hah! I hope you aren't about to pretend you've ever read any of my novels? I mean, all the way through?'

'What! Well, really, Paul, I won't even dignify that unforgivable slur with a reply.'

'I know you of old. You take ten per cent of my royalties and you read ten per cent of my books. If that.'

'Another lie! Hah, you old devil! You haven't changed a bit. But listen, listen. Even if I grant what you say is true – which I don't, mind you, not for an instant

I don't, but, okay, for the sake of the argument and to allow us to go on with this conversation – well, you still might have let me know what was in the offing.'

'Actually, Andrew, I did try to call you a few weeks ago.'

'So why didn't we speak?'

'You were away.'

'What? Out of the office?'

'No, away. Out of the country.'

'Out of the country? When did you say you tried to call?'

'Oh, two or three weeks ago.'

'Well, Paul, I don't know who you spoke to, or what you were told, but what with the new baby I haven't been out of the country since – ouf, it must be since Frankfurt last year.'

'What about your trip around the world?'

'My what?'

'Your trip around the world?'

'If only, old boy.'

'What?'

'Paul, I haven't been around the world. Ever.'

'Weren't you in Hong Kong? Australia? San Francisco?'

'Well, yes, I *have* been to all these places, but not all at once and not for years. Last time I was in San Francisco was with you, remember? In 19 – oh, 1990, I'd say.'

'Paul?'

'Paul? What is it?'

'Paul, what's that sound I hear?'
'That sound, Andrew, is the sound of scales falling from my sockets.'
'Falling from – ?'
'I'm going to hang up now, Andrew.'
'Paul? Paul, tell me what's going on? Suddenly you seem –'
'Forgive me. I'm going to have to go. And please don't try to contact me. Goodbye, Andrew.'
'Paul?'
'Goodbye.'

$$\sim$$

How could I have been so blind! Yes, blind! For now, as God is my witness, and as I am God's witness, now I am no longer playing with words. What a shallow, sentimental myth it is, that a blind man's functioning senses gradually learn to compensate for the loss of his sight! If some poor, filmy-eyed wild beast were as insensitive as I have been to all the signs with which I've been bombarded for the past month, it would not survive for long in this vale of tears. For there were so many signs after all, and I was so gullible! Oh, John Ryder, John Ryder, JohnRyder! I gave myself up to you as I would have done to my son, to my own prodigal son. No one blessed with eyes would have accorded you such licence. Yet I, eyeless, I opened my home to you, and you abused me, humiliated me, degraded me. A blind old man! Why? For Christ's sake, why? Who are you, John Ryder? Who are you? What is it you want of me? Are you some motiveless sadist who, as a child, enjoyed stripping the wings off flies and have now graduated to tormenting the old and blind and disabled? Or is it my money you hope to gain? Imposs- ible, ludicrous, preposterous. However this story is destined to end, that, you must know, you will never have. Then – my life? Again, why? What conceivable reason could you have for wanting the life of a lonely, defenceless old man? Oh God, I don't know! I don't know! And there's no one to whom I can turn for an answer. No one but you yourself, no one but the wretch that you are and that delights in strip- ping the wingsoff a blind man.

Well, so be it, John Ryder. If it's from you alone that enlight- enment comes, then so be it. We shall see what we shall see.

❧

'There you are.'

'Yeah.'

'Get everything you wanted?'

'Finally. It's uphill work in Chipping Campden. Shopping, I mean.'

'Is it really?'

'Everything all right here?'

'Oh. Fair, fair.'

'Why are you sitting in the study?'

'I really don't know. Waiting for you, I suppose.'

'Want me to make some coffee?'

'Not unless you yourself want some.'

'I had one in Chipping Campden.'

'Then shall we set to?'

'Is something the matter, Paul?'

'Why should anything be the matter?'

'Okay. I'll switch on.'

'Need to be reminded where we left off?'

'Don't bother.'

'No?'

'No. While you were out, you see, I had an idea.'

'Ah.'

'A brilliant idea, if I say so myself. I don't yet know, to be honest, where it's going to fit into the book – though, given how disjointed the structure has been so far, that's of no consequence in itself. I expect it'll find its place in the scheme of things. But I do believe that when one gets an idea this good it ought to be put to use as rapidly as possible.'

'Sounds exciting.'

'We can only hope.'

'Shall I create a new document?'

'Why not? It *is* a new departure.'

'What'll we call it?'

'Well, you know, John, I was thinking, just for this section, that I might revive the title I dropped a couple of weeks ago. You remember, the title I originally planned to give the whole book? *Truth and Consequences*?'

'Good idea. I'll just call it *Consequences*, then, shall I? Unless you find that too hard to live up to?'

'No. No, *Consequences* is fine. And, as you'll see, really rather appropriate.'

'Okay. I've already typed it in. Ready when you are.'

'All right. I'm starting – *now*. "It was Thomas Mann" – two n's, by the way.'

'Yes, thank you, Paul, I fancy I knew that already.'

'"It was Thomas Mann who once defined a writer as" – open quotes – 'someone for whom writing is more difficult than it is for other people'." Close quotes. "One knows, even if one is not a writer oneself, what he means. Yet definitions, aphoristic definitions, constitute what might be termed a genre and one of the absolutely immutable properties of that genre is that each definition in question be invested with what might be called an allure of improbability, even of paradox. It must, in short, be aback-taking." That's "aback" – hyphen – "taking".'

'Uh huh.'

'"In the case of Mann's definition, for example, a far more sensible formulation would be, as we are all secretly aware, that a writer is someone for whom writing is *less* difficult than it is for other people." Italicize "less". "Yet, had Mann actually made such a statement, then no one would of course have thought it worth quoting." Full stop. "And, to be fair, since mining one's way to a pertinent paradox, which is what he did, is inherently more difficult than parroting a near-tautologous platitude, which is what I have just done, it could be argued that his definition of a writer is a nicely self-illustrating example of what it in fact proposes." Ah, repetition there. Change the earlier "for example" to "for instance".'

'Changed.'

'I'm going on now. "In any event, whenever a writer defines a writer, he cannot do other than define himself" – dash – "not just in a generic but in an exclusively subjective sense. Mann's definition thus cannot be made to apply to Henry James" – semi-colon – "just as Henry James's would be unlikely to apply to, say, Ronald Firbank" – F, i, r, b, a, n, k – "nor Ronald Firbank's to me."'

'Would you like a second semi-colon? Between "Firbank" and "nor"?'

'I'll tell you when I want a semi-colon.'

'So how should I punctuate it?'

'I said nothing and nothing is what I want. No semi-colon, no colon, no comma. Is that understood?'

'Paul, have I –'

'I'm going on. "Take my own case. I am blind. Not only am I blind, I have no eyes. Hence –"'

'Paul?'

'What is it now?'

'Well, only that – well, I just thought I ought to point out that the very first sentence you ever dictated to me for the book was "I am blind".'

'*And*? In your opinion, *and*?'

'It's the repetition, that's all. You're usually so strict about repetition. I just wondered if you'd noticed? Or maybe you'd forgotten?'

'You were wondering if I'd noticed I was blind? If I'd forgotten I was blind? Is that what you were wondering?'

'Answer me. Is that what you're saying?'

'You know that's not what I'm saying.'

'I know nothing of the kind.'

'All I said was that you were repeating yourself. I may not be much of a literary critic, but I simply felt I should point out the repetition. That's all.'

'You're right.'

'Well, thanks.'

'You're not much of a literary critic.'

'How dare you. How dare you offer me advice on how I should or shouldn't write my book. How dare you "remind" me – me! – that I'm repeating myself. Repeating myself? As though repetition, premeditated repetition, were not one of the most venerable stylistic tropes to which a writer may have recourse. "My love is like a red, red rose" – get rid of that second "red", Rabbie Burns, you rank amateur you, you piddling mediocrity, can't you see you're repeating yourself! You forget yourself, Ryder. Frankly, I don't know what mail-order course in creative writing you once subscribed to, but I'm not about to be given a lesson in the nuances and niceties of literary style by a second-hand car salesman.'

'By a *what*?'

'Or whatever you are. Can you really suppose that your opinion of my prose matters a jot to me? I shall write "I am blind" as often as I think fit. And you will type it out on that infernal machine of yours and keep your night-class insights to yourself.'

'Very well. Very well, I'll do that.'

'Good.'

'But, before I do – before I do – I'm going to make one last comment.'

'If you must.'

'In my opinion, you make too much of your eyes.'

'I beg your pardon?'

'You make too much of your eyes. What you call your eyelessness. In the book – and, when I think of it, in person, too.'

'Now just –'

'What I'm about to say, and I know you won't agree with it, and I also know it's going to sound smug and sanctimonious, but what I'm about to say I believe I'm saying for your own good. And if it means you decide to dismiss me on the spot, well, so be it. I'll have said what I thought, and I won't regret it. You make too much of your eyes, Paul. You make too many self-deprecating little witticisms about your blindness. Too many puns, too many jokes. Yeah, yeah, at first it's all very impressive, this ability you have to shrug off your own predicament. You think, my God, if I had his problems, could I be that brave? But I have to tell you, Paul, it wears off. Christ, does it wear off! It becomes tiresome and mechanical and you begin to dread the next little wink and the next little eye-joke and you begin to think it would be better if he actually did whinge. That at least would be, I don't know, it would be sane. Healthy. Human.'

'There. That's all I wanted to say. The ball's back in your court.'

'I'm going on. Ready?'

'Yes.'

'"Take my own case. I am blind. Not only am I blind, I have no eyes. Hence any insight" – dash – "an odd word in the circumstances" – dash – "that I might offer my readers into the writer's condition and vocation cannot but be influenced by that flatly terrifying fact. And, plunged as I am in the endless nocturnality" – n, o, c, t, u, r, n, a, l, i, t, y – "which my life has become, I have had time to reflect a great deal on the strangely intimate correspondence that exists between blind-ness and fiction." Full stop.'

'Uh huh.'

'"For one day" – dash – "indeed, this very day, the day on which I am writing, or rather dictating, the pas-sage that you, the reader, are reading" – dash – "one day –"'

'I assume the repetition of "one day" is deliberate?'

'"One day it struck me that the blind man gains access to the world around him exactly as the reader of a novel gains access to the imaginative world conjured up by the writer." Full stop. "Which is to say, essentially through dialogue and description." Italicize "essentially through dialogue and description".'

'Done.'

'"Consider." Full stop. "The reader can know nothing of the milieu in which a novel is set except for that rigidly restricted zone, that prescribed and proscribed precinct" – that's "p – r – e -scribed" followed by "p – r – o -scribed" followed by "p – r – e -cinct".'

'Right.'

'"That prescribed and proscribed precinct, that codified plot of fictional terrain, of which the writer deigns to apprise him. If the writer, who may have his own good reasons, elects to leave the outward aspect of his settings or characters sketchy in the extreme, then that is all the reader is ever destined to know of them. He cannot peek over the tops of the words on the page, as he might endeavour to peek over the bobbing heads of a crowd of sightseers goggling at a passing parade, in order to get a better view of the world beyond them, for there is of course no world beyond." New paragraph. "Similarly with dialogue. It is above all, perhaps, through exchanges of dialogue that the reader comes to know the characters in a work of fiction. Only if the author elects to assume a first-person voice in his own narrative, by the device of an interior monologue, is that same reader granted privileged

access to the intimate mindset, to the moods and motivations, of any one character." Read those last two
sentences back to me, please.'

'"It is above all, perhaps, through exchanges of dialogue that the reader comes to know the characters in a
work of fiction. Only if the author elects to assume a
first-person voice in his own narrative, by the device
of an interior monologue, is that same reader granted
privileged access to the intimate mindset, to the
moods and motivations, of any one character."'

'New paragraph. "Consider, now, the blind man.
Like the reader of a novel, he, too, if he is ever to gain a
meaningful purchase on the otherwise inaccessible
world around him, will find himself totally dependent
upon the two most prominent stylistic parameters of
the traditional novelistic discourse" – dash – "description and dialogue. By description, I mean the running
commentary offered the blind man by some real-life
narrator, some companion, perhaps, either paid or
unpaid, who takes his arm, figuratively but also literally, and whose role is to describe to him the shifting
spectacle of the external world just as a commentator
might describe the progress of a cricket match on the
wireless. And, by dialogue, I refer to the fact that, as
with the reader of conventional fiction, it is primarily
by virtue of what they have to say, either to him or to
each other, that the blind man understands the psy-

chology of those in with whom" – yes, "in with whom" – "he has thrown his social and emotional lot." End of paragraph.'

'Are you still with me, John?'
'Of course.'
'For a while there it seemed to me you'd stopped typing.'
'I've been typing throughout.'
'Good. Then I'll go on. Did I say a new paragraph?'
'Yes, you did.'
'"Both reader and blind man, then, rely absolutely on the accuracy and sincerity" – emphasize "sincerity".'

'Do you mean italicize it?'
'Yes, I do. I'm going on. "The accuracy and *sincerity* of the information communicated to them by, respectively, the writer and the paid companion. If, however, either said writer or said paid companion should prove to be less than wholly reliable, then they are both of them, reader and blind man, marooned in the dark."

'John?'
'Yes?'
'You *are* getting this, are you?'
'Yes, yes. Go on.'

'I must be going deaf. Or else you've become an extraordinarily discreet typist.'

'Very well, I'm going on. "The issue is by no means a purely theoretical one, of interest solely to critics and scholars. Bizarre paradox as it may appear, a writer is capable of lying" – emphasize "lying" – "a writer is capable of *lying* in a work of fiction" – colon – "the examples are legion, notably in the current postmodern era. Here, however, my analogy with the condition of the blind man breaks down, or so at least one trusts. Certainly, it would be hard – it would be hard – it would be *very* hard – to conceive of the imaginary companion whom I have described above deliberately choosing to lie" – emphasize "lie" – deliberately choosing to *lie* to a blind man about the realities of the world which he is supposed, and has doubtless been handsomely paid, to describe. What would one think of a –"'

'Now, John, you *really* aren't taking any of this down. I can hear. I mean, I can't hear. I can't hear any typing at all.'

'What's the matter? Cat got your finger?'

'You can be surprisingly unsubtle, you know, Paul.'
'Can I?'

'I mean to say, for a great writer, Booker Prizewinner, Grand Old Man of English Letters, all that crap, your methods are sometimes amazingly crude.'

'You, John Ryder, are a crude antagonist.'

'May I ask why you're laughing?'

'I'm laughing because I've finally found the perfect title for your book. *Blind Man's Bluff*. Don't suppose you'd care for it, though. Sounds too much like a Jeffrey Archer.'

'You're a cool one, I must say.'

'Am I?'

'Yes, you're a cool bastard.'

'And why is that?'

'What I've just dictated to you? It never occurred to you that it might represent my considered reflections on certain general principles of literary theory and practice?'

'No, it didn't.'

'No, it didn't. You immediately, *immediately*, presumed it had to do with the – with the – the palpable tension between us. Not only that. Without further proof, without a shred of corroborating evidence, you instantly exposed your own hand. Yes, I call that cool.'

'Why waste time?'

'You could have been giving yourself away prematurely.'

'I knew I wasn't giving anything away. I know you too well. Though, just out of curiosity, Paul, who or what tipped you off?'

'I spoke to Andrew.'

'Who?'

'Andrew Boles. My agent. I rang him up while you were in Chipping Campden.'

'Aha. I see. And he –'

'I naturally enquired about his trip around the world.'

'I see. I see. Now that *was* foolish of me. I just didn't imagine you were capable of using the phone. So you told him about me, did you?'

'Actually, no. I didn't. I could have, but for some reason I didn't. Probably because I had – and I still have – no idea what this is all about.'

'The word is "should", Paul, not "could".'

'What?'

'You *should* have told him about me, you really should. Funny. I feel almost sorry for you.'

'Oh, and why?'

'Because now it's too late for you to do anything at all.'

'Who are you, John Ryder?'

'Who am I? Aha. That's a question I've been waiting a month to hear you ask me.'

'I don't understand.'
'No?'

'Or maybe I do. Maybe I *am* starting to understand.'

'You *are* someone, aren't you?'

'I mean, you're someone I know?'

'Someone I've known a lot longer than a month?'

'Well? Aren't you?'

'Answer me, for Christ's sake!'
'Yes, Paul, I'm someone you know.'
'Someone I know. Or someone I used to know?'
'It's a small world, Paul. Especially if you're blind.'

'All right. All right now. I'm determined to stay perfectly calm. I may be blind, but I can still think and I can still talk. *We* can talk, can't we?'

'Yes. Yes, all right, John. There's something going on here I don't fully grasp. But what I suspect – well, what I suspect is that you're someone with a grievance against me? Am I right?'

'If that's the case, if that *is* the case, John, then we can talk about it. We can always talk about it. You can tell me what – what I did, if it *was* something I did, and we can talk about it, can't we? John?'

'Say something! Anything!'

'Yes, Paul. We're going to talk about it. Or rather, I'm going to talk about it and you're going to sit and listen.'
'I'd rather stand if you don't mind.'
'You'll fucking sit. Sit down or I'll throw you down!'
'What!'
'Don't think I wouldn't! Just to shut you up I would!'

'That's it. Now. Now. Now, Paul, you're going to listen to me for a change.'

'You know, Paul, you're unbelievable. I just can't believe what I've had to take from you this past month. "Make yourself at home, John." "Don't forget the semi-colon, John." "Why didn't you laugh at my little joke, John?" "We'll be having cocktails at seven, John." Just who the fuck do you think you are?'
'Must you use that language?'
'Shut up! I can't fucking bear the sound of your

voice! You say another fucking word, so help me, I'll stick my fist right down your fucking throat!'

'Good. Now I'm going to tell you a story – *my* story, for a change – and if you're willing to sit and listen to it without interrupting me, I'll try not to use too many of these nasty four-letter words you're so squeamish about all of a sudden. Okay?'

'A little while ago, Paul, when you lost your temper with me, you said – and I quote – "You forget yourself." Well, now it's my turn to make a little joke, because you couldn't have got it more hopelessly wrong. No, Paul. I didn't forget myself. *I remembered myself.* I remembered myself at the age of eleven. Do you by any chance remember me at the age of eleven?'

'No need to start racking those great big bulging brains of yours. I mean to remind you.'

'So. I was eleven. Eleven years old. An ordinary schoolkid. Well, no, it's true, not an ordinary schoolkid. I was in a special school, a school for difficult children, violent children, the sort no other school, no "nice" school, wanted to know about. A school for kids who'd been expelled from everywhere else.'

'Though I must say in all fairness it wasn't a bad school in its way. It had a football pitch, a rugby pitch, indoor swimming-pool, lots of nice big dormitories. Just outside Chichester. Aha! Is it starting to come back?'

'Oh God!'

'Why, Paul, you *do* remember me. Or do you? Maybe there were just too many of us for you to remember one particular boy? Especially because it was all so long ago, twenty-two years ago. Imagine, Paul, twenty-two years. Makes you think, doesn't it? You weren't a world-famous author in those days, were you? Just a couple of novels no one had paid any attention to. Am I right?'

'Yes, just another poor underpaid schoolmaster. English and physical education. How many boys were you responsible for? Thirty? Forty? We should hold a class reunion one of these days, me and the boys. Talk over old times.'

'But, you know, Paul, I still can't help flattering myself I was your special favourite. "My little cherub", you used to call me, "my little angel-face". Teacher's pet, that was me. Teacher's little pet that teacher liked to stroke and cuddle and fondle and kiss, remember? *Do* you remember, Paul?'

'Oh God, stop it, will you! Stop it!'

'Hah! It *is* a small world. You know why I say that, Paul? You know why? Because those were the exact same words I screamed out all those years ago. "Stop it, will you! Stop it!" I can still hear myself, I can still hear those screams bouncing against the walls of the gym. But no one else could hear me, could they? Just as no one else can hear you now.'

'Remember, Paul? Remember what you liked best?'

'You liked to pull your cock out, remember? Do you? And then you'd take hold of my two hands, my two little hands –'

'Stop it! For Christ's sake, stop it!'

'Shut up!'

'You'd take hold of my hands and then you got me to guide it, your great big fleshy red cock, it was a real monster in those days, wasn't it, not like the pathetic drippy thing that dangles between your legs now, and you got me to guide it into my mouth, and I could hardly get my mouth open wide enough. Wasn't that cute? You used to find that so fucking cute. You liked the word "cute", I remember, it was a word you used a lot. And then, and then, when your cock was right inside my mouth and I'd just about stopped breathing

– I wanted to throw up – you'd pull down my under-pants, my soggy grey little Y-fronts. Oh, they were cute too, weren't they so fucking cute, those little grey Y-fronts of mine? So cute you used to rub your nose in them, remember? And then you'd take my balls in your hands, my cute little balls, and you'd squeeze them so hard I wanted to scream my head off, but I couldn't, could I, because I had your cock half-way down my throat, your big dribbling red raw cock, and you were squeezing my balls harder and harder till you came right inside my mouth.'

'And do you remember what you did then? Do you? Oh, this was wonderful, this was the best of all. You'd quickly draw your cock out of my mouth and then I *would* throw up, I couldn't help it, ever, and I used to see your face when you made me barf all over your cock, I used to see it, Paul, and I can tell you, at that moment your face was even more of a horror than it is now.'

'Oh God, oh God, oh God.'

'It's all wrong, I know. For *A Closed Book*, I mean. Subject-matter's all wrong. After all those high-falutin ramblings of yours about eyes and blindness and eye-lessness, it would come as too big a shock to the reader's system. Yeah, but that's life, you see, Paul.

You said it yourself, remember? Life doesn't stick to the rules. It springs the sort of climax on you that you don't expect.'

'Oh Jesus, what are you going to do?'

'First, Paul, I'm going to go on with my story. You didn't know I tried to kill myself, did you? With a razor. No, of course you didn't. That was after you'd left the school. After you'd given up your job. *Sitting at the Feet of Ghosts*, wasn't it? A big, big success. The Booker Prize. Christ knows how many editions. Big-budget Hollywood movie. You didn't need me any longer. You didn't need any of us. Besides . . . besides, you were getting to be a bit too well-known, weren't you? A bit too conspicuous. If you wanted some little tyke to vomit over your cock, you had to start travelling, moving around a bit. Like – like Sri Lanka, no?'

'I moved around a bit too. In my own way. In and out of reform schools, sleeping in the streets, that sort of moving around. Always on my own, always. Because I never could trust anyone. Never.'

'What? No comment, Paul? Words fail you for once? Never mind, I'm just going to go on anyway. And actually, Paul, you'll be surprised to hear that my story lightens up a bit now. You wouldn't think it could, would you, but it does. Because I met this guy. Nothing out of the ordinary. Just a nice enough guy on the streets like me, Chris was his name, and we started bunking down together a lot of the time. Then one day, hallelujah, Chris landed himself a job. Teaching English. Just like you. Is that spooky or what? Teaching English in a crummy language school off Regent Street, sort of bargain-basement Berlitz, was what he told me, a total rip-off. You see, Chris turned out to be really quite well educated, I don't know how he got to be on the streets, I never asked him and he never told me, but, anyway, he got this job and he rented a flat and I moved in with him. A council flat in the East End.'

'Well, we lived there together for a bit. And one day I was sitting alone in Chris's flat and I said to myself – I said to myself – if he can do it, I can do it. You know? I can get my act together too. And that's when I changed my name – changed it to John Ryder. It wasn't any sort of precaution, you understand. I didn't know then I'd be standing over you now. It's just that I was in the process of remaking myself, reinventing myself, and it felt good to have a new name for the new me.'

'So, as I say, I got myself a job, any job, anything I

could find, working in a video shop, a betting shop, selling fruit and veg in a Bermondsey street market, you name it, you can bet I did it. And then, finally, to cut a long story short, I got myself hired as a runner in a brokerage firm in the City. Office boy, basically, but I was smarter than most of them there and I even did a bit of trading on my own, just penny shares, but I was really very good at it, so good I realized I could do better for myself if I did it from home. Which is what I've been doing for the last eight years. Till I turned up on your doorstep.'

'Still nothing to say? Nah, it's not the kind of story that appeals to you. Not what you'd call "postmodern", is it? Too much gritty realism. Touch of the Irving Welshes. Not your sort of thing at all.'

'You didn't expect me to know a fancy word like "postmodern", did you? Well, but you see, Paul, it's you I have to thank. You see, you forgot me, but I didn't forget you. I *never* forgot you. I read your novels. I read your interviews. I saw the movie. I even watched the Oscar night ceremony on TV. Tough luck, Paul. Best Costume Design. Better than a kick in the pants, I suppose.'

'I was like a stalker – an invisible stalker. Because

nowadays, as I discovered, you can be a stalker without stepping outside your own home. That's how I
stalked you – on TV, through the newspapers, through
magazines. It was easy. It was child's play. You were so
famous, Paul, you'd become so fucking ubiquitous. Is
that the word? Ubiquitous?'

'The Booker. The Whitbread. Your knighthood.
Everything you did, I watched you do. Everywhere
you went, I went too. Invisible but I was right beside
you. And then one day, one day – wham! – Booker
Prizewinning Author in Near-Fatal Car Crash in Sri
Lanka.'

'Now, Paul, here comes the funny bit. Because you
might have thought I'd be over the moon about that
crash of yours. I wasn't, though. No, no, no, no, no!
That wasn't what I called revenge. Maybe it was God's
revenge. Maybe it was good enough for God. It wasn't
good enough for me.'

'No, no, your crash was bad news for me. Because
suddenly there was nothing. Nothing about you anywhere. Nothing to tell me whether you were still in Sri
Lanka or over here or somewhere else altogether.
There was a time there, Paul, I thought I'd lost you for
good. I thought it was all over for me, I really did. Till

the day, oh and it was the most marvellous, the most exquisite day in my entire life, till the day I opened *The Times* and I noticed, I just noticed it, Paul, I came *that* close to not noticing it, till the day I saw your ad.'

'Oh, it was a subtle one. No name. No identification. Just the two words "blind author". No, no, no, I tell a lie. What you wrote was "sightless author", wasn't it? "Sightless author seeks amanuensis." And I knew, I *knew*, it just had to be you. And I thought, now I've got him! Now I've got him! Now I'm going to be his amanufuckingensis!'

'What are you going to do to me?'
'Wait, wait, wait. It's not over yet. I've left the best for last.'

'We've been working hard on that book of yours, haven't we? What is it you like to call it? Your testament? Well, I tell you, Paul, you don't know how right you are. It *is* going to be your testament. But you know the best joke of all, Paul? You do, don't you? You must have guessed by now?'

'It was from Chris I got the idea. Remember Chris? Taught English in a language school? TEFL. Teaching English as a Foreign Language.'

'Well, he used to talk to me about it. How he'd have a class of pupils from all over the place, German businessmen, Japanese students, I don't know, Brazilian interpreters, whole mishmash of nationalities, and the only language they were allowed to speak was English. Right from the start, right from the very first session. Total Immersion, they called it. Even in the beginners' class, bunch of forty students, not one of them with a word of English to his name, except "yes", "no", "okay", "Coca-Cola", and he'd have to teach them the language from scratch. And you know what he told me? He told me that, sometimes, when he went into that beginners' class he'd have this fantasy about teaching them not English at all but *a completely invented language*! You understand? He'd fantasize about making up words of his own the night before, words for "me" and "you" and "come" and "go" and "table" and "chair", these would be the words he'd teach them, and none of them would know any better, and by the end of the course there they'd all be, yammering away to each other, really, really fluently, but in a language that didn't exist! Wouldn't that have been something? He used to imagine them all returning home, back to Germany or Japan, really satisfied with the course, and the very next day they'd walk into some high-powered business conference and they'd open their big mouths and start spouting this completely invented language! God, we laughed!'

'I'm smiling at it now. Can you hear me, Paul? Can you hear me smile?'

'Anyway, for Chris it was just a fantasy. But I never forgot it. And when I came here I thought I'd give it a go for real. And that's why your book's a joke, Paul. Because everything in it, and I mean absolutely everything, is gibberish.'

'I can hear the critics now. Tragic case – premature senility – Alzheimer's – mind destroyed by his terrible accident. The Rembrandt – the statue of Diana – Hertford College – St Paul's – the Millennium Dome – the Burger King on Hampstead Heath. Oh, I could go on and on and on. Isaiah Berlin's dead not alive, Pete Townshend's alive not dead, Tony Blair, Saddam Hussein, O. J. Simpson, Salman Rushdie, Martin Amis – your book, Paul, your book is a monstrosity, it's a folly, it's a joke, it's as big a freak as you yourself are, it's nothing but the incontinent ravings of a doddering, gibbering old fart!'

'Oh please God!'

'Why don't you pretend you're having a nightmare, Paul? Isn't that what you used to say to me? Remember?

"Just pretend you're having a nightmare, angel-face."'

'Listen, John, listen to me. Please God, listen to me. I wronged you, I know. What I did to you was a terrible, terrible thing, I can never take it back , never, but – but look, you're – what I mean is, I'm rich, John, I'm a wealthy man, a very wealthy man, I can make it up to you, no, no, no, of course I can't, I'll never be able to do that, but – but you're young, you've got your life ahead of you, and I can make that life worth living, I can, I mean it, John, I'll give you – I'll turn my entire fortune over to you, everything, you'll have every-thing, only – John, are you listening? John, are you lis-tening to me?'

'John?'

'John? Where are you?'

'Please, John, don't do this to me, please. Not to a poor old blind man.'

'What are you doing, John? Oh, God, pleaaaffff-phm –'

'There there, Paul. Not too tight, I hope. No, no, seems okay.'

'Don't worry. You won't have it on for long.'

'Ooops. Oh, I'm sorry. I seem to have knocked your glasses off and – oh dear, now I've trod on them too. Tsk tsk. Butterfingers. No, I suppose I mean butter-feet.'

'It doesn't matter anyway. You won't need dark glasses in hell.'

'Now, Paul, let me explain why you have that strip of Scotch tape across your mouth. It's a temporary measure, you understand, I'll be taking it off again before you know it. I've no desire to leave any tell-tale signs of our, shall I say, our little falling-out. And don't think it's because I'm afraid someone will hear you. In this lonely old house of yours, as you yourself are well aware, Paul, there *is* no one who can hear you.'

'It's just that I want you to know exactly what's about to happen to you and if you began to scream, you see, you might not hear what I have to say.'

'Strange. Your mouth has been gagged. And you have no eyes. Yet I can still detect the fear in your face.'

'Oh, but I can't stand here for ever, just gazing at you, wonderful as such a prospect would be. As I was about to say, what I had in mind from the very beginning – from our very first meeting – was of course to kill you. That, I'm sure, you've already figured out for yourself. The problem, though, was finding a method. You see, I was determined that the punishment would fit the crime. Or, anyway, fit the criminal. And you can be sure I had no intention of being punished myself. So it was something I had to think long and hard about. And then one day it came to me. That was the day we were in your bedroom going through your ties. Oh, and by the way, Paul, you remember the tie with the stain on it, the tie you thought was a Cerruti? Well – oh, but you know perfectly well what I'm going to say, don't you?'

'I'll say it anyway, just in case. It *was* the Cerruti and there *was* no stain. Just another of my little jokes.'

'I know, I know, you don't have to tell me, it was idiotic, it was infantile. Like most of those little jokes of mine. But it was great fun while it lasted and, well, you have to build up to a climax very, very gradually.'

'Anyway, there we both were, you and I, rummaging through your ties, and I suddenly thought to myself, my, but this is a spacious wardrobe. So spacious, I thought, you could actually stand right inside it. Of course, you couldn't move around too much. And you'd have to be a bit careful about breathing. All the same –'

'Uh-uh-uh, Paul. Naughty, naughty. No struggling, now. Just sit there quietly or I'll have to pin you down.'

'The only thing was, if I were to stick you in there, well, even you could get out of that wardrobe. And locking the door from the outside wasn't a solution either, for obvious reasons. Still, I liked the feel of the idea and I wasn't ready to give it up and I thought about it and I thought about it until finally, just this morning as it happens, I found the answer. The door. The door that keeps swinging open. This morning you walked into it again, and you've walked into it before, even Mrs Kilbride knows that, which, incidentally, will come in useful when the police start to snoop around. Oh, and again by the way, Paul, I think you ought to know, just to keep you right up to date, poor old Joe Kilbride genuinely *is* ill. Believe it or not, that wasn't one of my lies. It was just my good fortune, just a pure stroke of luck. I deserved at least one, don't you think?'

'So, anyway, now we come to the nitty-gritty. My story – to the police, I mean – is that you asked me to change the spring on that door, which is what I'm going to do this very day. I *did* buy one of those restrictor things – you remember, I told you about them, they make doors slam shut when you let them go, and, well, I bought one this morning at the locksmith's in Chipping Campden and I plan to fix it to the inside of the wardrobe door. It shouldn't take me more than half-an-hour or so. Then, this weekend, when I drive back to London, and you're completely alone, you're going to go looking for a tie inside that wardrobe, one of your elegant Charvet ties – then, hey, hey, what *is* this, the tie hanger seems to be right at the back. Fuck it, I can hear you say in that inimitable way you have, fuck it, who's been moving my ties? And then, because you've got to have your tie, you wouldn't be you if you weren't wearing a tie, without thinking, completely forgetting the spring's been changed in the meantime, you step right inside the wardrobe to get the tie and, hey presto, the door snaps shut behind you!'

'I'll have left you something to eat in the kitchen. A plate of cold cuts, I think, and a bottle of Rioja. No one will come calling. No one will hear you scream. No one but you. And the darkness. And the silence.'

'You'll be locked inside that wardrobe, Paul, just the way you might be locked inside the pages of a book. A closed book.'

'I won't leave you inside for too long. To be on the safe side, what I'll do is drive back down on Sunday morning. That should be time enough. And to be on the *extra*-safe side, I've decided to line the outside of the wardrobe with some of this thick Scotch tape. I'm counting on your claustrophobia to do the trick, but just in case it doesn't, I'm going to take the extra precaution of cutting off all your air. Almost all your air, I dare say it won't be totally airtight.'

'Then, on Sunday morning, I'll strip it off again, open the door and – well, God knows what I'll find. Not a pretty sight, I imagine. But to me, Paul, to me it'll be a masterpiece.'

'So there it is, the end of my little tale. I've got it off my chest and all that's left for me now is to get it out of my system.'

'Now, Paul, what I intend to do is take you upstairs with me. You understand? I'd rather have you at my side while I fix the door, I'd prefer to have you where I can keep an eye on you. Yeah, yeah, yeah, I know what you're trying to tell me. A blind man can't get into too much trouble by himself. It's true. But it's just the way I am, cautious to a fault.'

'So – so just let me take you by the arm – that's it – now don't resist, Paul, please don't resist – it's going to happen anyway whatever you do. That's right – just fall limp, like that – good – good – good – makes it all the easier for both of us. All right, now, one foot in front of the other – right foot first – now the left – there's a good boy – *there's* a good boy – at this rate we'll be at the stairs in a jiffy – no, no, no, don't panic – I've got you – I've got you – I promise I won't let go – just try to stand upright – that's it – *that's* it – good, very good – now the other leg – good – you're doing just fine – good – good – good – that's it – good, Paul, very, very good . . .'

❧

'Mr Ryder? Mr John Ryder?'
    'Yes?'
    'I'm Inspector Truex. I believe you were advised I'd be calling?'
    'Oh yes. Yes, of course. Come in, come in.'
    'Thanks. We'll try not to take up too much of your time.'
    'Not at all. I understand. This way. Yes, in fact, I was told. Yes. In here'll be best, I think.'

'Ah, thank you.'

'Hmm. Interesting room, isn't it? A real writer's room.'

'Well, yes, I suppose it is. Though, actually, most of the writing was done next door. In the study. Sir Paul's study. Please. Please take a seat. And you too – ?'

'Forgive me. This is Sergeant Gillespie.'

'How do you do, Sergeant?'

'How d'you do, sir?'

'Hah, snap! Please, you too, Sergeant, take a seat. Now. Is there anything I can get you? Something to drink?'

'Well, sir, that's very kind of you, but we won't, thanks. You know what they say on TV? Not while we're on duty.'

'Ah, so you're on duty, then?'

'Well, yes, naturally we are. Nothing to be alarmed about, though. All just routine.'

'Which they also say on TV.'

'So they do, sir, so they do. Anyway, there are a few questions that have always got to be asked in these – these unfortunate cases. We could have had this conversation down at the station, but I thought you'd prefer to have it at home. I hope you don't mind?'

'Not at all. I'm extremely grateful. But you really shouldn't refer to this cottage as my home. I was just

Sir Paul's employee. Nothing here belongs to me.'

'Is that why you're packing, sir?'

'How did you know I was packing?'

'The window seat? The little pile of neatly folded shirts?'

'Very observant of you, Inspector. It's true, I am packing. Most of my luggage is still upstairs. Now that Sir Paul – well, as I said, there's absolutely nothing to keep me here a day longer.'

'You aren't one of his beneficiaries?'

'Me? Good Lord, no.'

'Stranger things have happened.'

'No, no. Sir Paul paid me by the month. Paid me well, too. But there was no question of his leaving me anything. I've never for a moment entertained such an idea.'

'How long have you been with him? Had you been with him, I should say?'

'Just over a month. And I've been paid up to date. No complaints on that score.'

'And you're going – ?'

'Going?'

'May I ask where you're going? I mean, now?'

'Oh. Back to my house in London. You know, Inspector, I've already given my London address to the police.'

'Please, Mr Ryder, it's not a problem. Just my natural nosiness.'

'I *can* leave, can't I? I mean, I don't have to report to anyone, do I?'

'Absolutely not. No, no, no. You may go whenever you like.'

'So what exactly can I do for you?'

'Well, I'll tell you, Mr Ryder. There seems to be no doubt at all as to what happened. It's a very nasty case indeed. Death by accident – apparently from suffocation. But in all such cases, especially with a man as prominent as Sir Paul was, we've still got to go through the motions. There'll be an inquest of course. But, as you can imagine, it's my job to make sure nothing's been overlooked.'

'I'll do my best to answer whatever questions you have.'

'Well now, it was you who discovered Sir Paul's body, was it not?'

'Yes. I found him upstairs. In his bedroom wardrobe.'

'Forgive me, Mr Ryder, but how did – well, how did you know he was there? I mean, he'd got himself locked inside the wardrobe, hadn't he?'

'That's right.'

'And he'd already been dead for some hours?'

'Yes, he had.'

'So how did you know where to look?'

'By the smell, I'm afraid.'

'The smell?'

'Listen, Inspector, I told everything I know to the policeman who – you know, when I called the police?'

'If you wouldn't mind, sir.'

'Oh, okay. Well, when I got back – I'd been in London for the weekend – I looked just about everywhere for him and, well, you know, he couldn't have gone anywhere – by himself, I mean – so I went back into his bedroom and I happened to walk close by the wardrobe and it was then, well, I suddenly smelt . . . Poor man, he'd soiled himself.'

'Hmm. Pretty grim for you.'

'Inspector, that was the least of it. His face – never, never in my life, will I forget the look of sheer – the look of petrified – kind of *frozen* – horror on his face. And his hands –'

'What about his hands?'

'He'd obviously been clawing away at the door. His fingernails were completely raw – his fingers caked with blood – all ten of them – skin scraped down to the bone – just red meat. It was horrible.'

'Uh huh.'

'So you'd been away?'

'Well, yes. As I say, it was the weekend. I tend not to stay here at weekends. I drive up to London and usually return – returned – on Sunday evening. Sometimes first thing Monday morning.'

'But in fact it was on the Sunday morning that you found his body?'

'That's right. I came back earlier, for some reason.'

'For some reason? Was there a reason?'

'No, not really. I was a bit bored in London, I found myself at a loose end, so I thought I might just as well drive back down. I suppose you could say I'd come to feel at home here. A month is quite a long time. My life had got completely wrapped up in Sir Paul's.'

'You were helping him write a book, is that it?'

'Yeah. He had decided to write what he called his testament. His literary testament. But given his condition –'

'He had no eyes?'

'He lost them, both of them, in a terrible car accident in Sri Lanka. Four years ago.'

'So he could see nothing at all?'

'He had no eyes, Sergeant.'

'Ah. Right.'

'Listen, Gillespie, why don't you take a quick look

round the cottage? Who knows, you might find something that'll give us a clue to Sir Paul's state of mind.
That is, if you have no objection, Mr Ryder?'

'I told you already, Inspector, I'm in no position to
object. This is not my house. I don't rightly know
whose it is now that Sir Paul's gone, but I certainly
can't stop you looking around. Not that I would anyway.'

'Do you happen to know if he died intestate?'

'Surely not. But, really, I've no idea.'

'Any relatives you're aware of?'

'We never spoke about his family.'

'I see, I see. Well, Sergeant, go on. Have a discreet
nose around.'

'Right, sir.'

'I realize all this must appear pointless to you, Mr
Ryder, but – well, you never can tell.'

'I made sure I touched as little as possible. That's
what you're supposed to do, isn't it?'

'With murder cases, yes, it's true. But, pooh, with an
accident like this. Go on, though. You were saying?'

'I'm sorry, what were we talking about?'

'Sir Paul was looking for someone to help him write
his book?'

'That's right. An amanuensis. Someone who'd tran-
scribe what he dictated. He put an ad in *The Times*, I

noticed it, I answered it and, I have to say, to my total surprise – frankly, I didn't think I had a hope in hell – but he seemed to take a shine to me and I've been more or less living down here ever since.'

'Pleasant work, was it?'

'You never met Sir Paul?'

'No, sir, I never had that privilege.'

'Well, I don't know that "pleasant" is the word I'd use. No, that's unfair. No, I have to say it was actually very rewarding.'

'Rewarding?'

'Yes, rewarding. To feel the book beginning to take shape and to realize that you're part of the shaping process. Yes, for someone like me that was very exciting.'

'Yes. Yes, I can see that it might be. To be honest with you, I've never actually read any of his novels myself. Stephen King is more in my line. Was this going to be a good one, in your opinion?'

'It wasn't a novel. It was to be a sort of autobiographical memoir.'

'Ah yes, of course. So you said.'

'And you have to appreciate that only a small part of it was ever written.'

'Even so. You must have formed some idea?'

'Well . . . what I *can* say is that there were strange things in the book, things Sir Paul insisted on keeping in even after I told him different. Not that I ever actually argued with him – I wouldn't have dared – but I have to say I never really understood what the point was.'

'Not quite with you here, sir. What sort of things are you referring to?'

'Oh, he'd get a bee in his bonnet about something, some fantastical notion that had no basis in fact but that he was nevertheless determined to use in his book. Symbolically, you might say.'

'For example?'

'Oh God, it's always hard to come up with specific examples. No, wait, I do remember one. The empty statue, the empty plinth, in Trafalgar Square. We had quite a discussion about that one, as I recall.'

'You'll have to explain, sir.'

'Well, as you know – or maybe you don't know, not being a Londoner – Trafalgar Square has four monumental plinths, one at each of its four corners. But, in fact, there are only three statues. The fourth one's unoccupied. Has been for decades. Well, anyway, Sir Paul had heard some vague rumour about how they might erect a statue to Diana – you know, after her car crash – and though it hasn't happened and, if you want my opinion, it's never going to happen, he insisted on writing about it as though it already had. There's a section in the book on Trafalgar Square and the National Gallery, don't ask why. Anyway, he insisted on writing about it as though it had already happened. As though the statue were already up. I won't say I tried to talk him out of it – it wasn't my place to argue with a great writer – but I did take the liberty of expressing – well, expressing certain misgivings about the whole idea and Paul took that rather badly. I was almost told to pack my bags there and then.'

'But you didn't.'

'No, he seemed to think twice about it. But the business about the statue stayed in. And the book, or what we wrote of it, has lots of other little – little anomalies, you might call them. I never objected again, as you can imagine. And probably, if we'd finished it and it'd been published, probably these would have been the very things the critics would have got most excited about.'

'Mmm. Funny lot, critics. Never read them myself. I somehow know in advance what I'm going to enjoy without anyone recommending it to me, know what I mean?'

'I know exactly what you mean.'

'So. Sir Paul was a bit cantankerous, was he?'

'He could be. He certainly could be. I had to laugh once.'

'At what?'

'Well, he once told me that, because of his blindness, he'd turned himself into what he liked to call "the salt of the earth". You know, being nice to everyone all the time, even if he didn't feel like it, because he was so dependent and he was afraid people wouldn't help him out if he wasn't very nice to them. The salt of the earth. Can you imagine? If that's what he called being the salt of the earth, God knows what he must have been like before his accident.'

'As difficult as that, was he?'

'Oh well, yes, at times. Other times, though, when he was on form, he could be very witty.'

'A bit of a raconteur?'

'Well, up to a point. He did have a habit of repeating himself. I used to hang on his every *other* word, as you might say.'

'Hah, yes. So he'd tend to blow hot and cold?'

'Exactly. But, you know, when you think about what had happened to him, you can't be too harsh. Personally, I'd have tried to kill myself.'

'Suicide? Not so easy without eyes.'

'True. But I'd have found a way.'

'It never crossed your mind that it might have *been* suicide?'

'What? Sir Paul's death?'

'Uh huh.'

'No way. Absolutely not.'

'Well, think of it, sir. None of the traditional avenues open to him – he gets desperate –'

'Take my word for it, Inspector. He didn't commit suicide.'

'How can you be so sure?'

'Because I knew him. Because one of the very first things he ever told me about himself was that he was mortally afraid of the dark.'

'Afraid of the dark? A blind man afraid of the dark?'

'I know. But that's what Sir Paul told me. He was incredibly claustrophobic. "I feel claustrophobic in the universe", that's how he put it. Of course, that was typical of him. Just one of his exaggerations. A lot of what he'd say was said purely for effect, you know. But, in fact, having got to know him as well as I did, I've come to the conclusion it was closer to the truth than it sounds.'

'Well, well, well.'

'But then, Mr Ryder, something occurs to me.'

'Yes?'

'Well, given what you've just been saying, it does seem odd he'd have such a powerful spring on his wardrobe door.'

'Odd?'

'Oh, odd that someone as claustrophobic as you say

he was would risk having happen to him what actually did happen to him in the end. I mean to say, the door springing shut and trapping him inside.'

'Yes, you're right . . . Yes, I never thought of that.'

'He probably didn't either. You'd be amazed how easygoing and thoughtless people can be when what's potentially at stake is their greatest fear in life. By the way, it looked fairly new.'

'What did?'

'The spring on the wardrobe door. It looked as though it had just been changed. It was a bit bloodstained, but you could tell it was new.'

'It *was* new. As a matter of fact, I was the one who changed it.'

'You were?'

'That's right.'

'At Sir Paul's request?'

'Naturally.'

'Why on earth did he want it changed?'

'I gather the catch had always been a bit faulty. The door didn't close properly and once or twice Sir Paul had walked into it. He hadn't realized it had swung back open and, you know, he'd hurt himself quite badly. Actually, he did it again only the other day. Walked smack into the side of the door. Given himself a big black-and-blue bruise. As I recall, you could still see it on his forehead.'

'Yes, we noticed that.'

'So, anyway, he was telling me about what had happened and I said, if he liked, I'd put a new spring in. What's called a restrictor. I'm quite good at that kind of odd job.'

'He specified that particular type, did he?'

'Yes, he did. I remember that clearly.'

'I see. So why do you suppose he actually stepped right inside the wardrobe, it being so narrow and him so claustrophobic?'

'There I can't help you, Inspector. Except –'

'Yes?'

'Well, as you can check for yourself, Sir Paul had a lot of clothes. A whole wardrobe. I got the impression he must have been quite a – quite a dapper sort of dresser before, well, before the disaster struck him. It's true, all the time I was with him, I never saw him wearing anything around the house but a slovenly old dressing-gown. The same dressing-gown he died in. Still, you could tell it had once been expensive. Fine silk and all. He'd let himself go, and who can blame him? But, anyway, as I say, he had lots of clothes, lots of suits and jackets, all made to measure, and he'd actually taken the trouble to memorize the exact order they were hung up in the wardrobe. So I can only suppose he stepped right inside the thing to get out some jacket or maybe a tie – he was very proud of his collection of ties – maybe a tie hanging up at the far end.'

'Sounds reasonable. Except, if you say he never wore anything but a ratty old dressing-gown, why go to all the trouble of hunting out something special? For whose benefit?'

'He always did wear a tie. Always. Even when he hadn't shaved for a couple of days, you could be sure he'd have one of his silk ties on.'

'Did he ever have visitors?'

'No.'

'What, never?'

'In the month I've been here, not one person ever came to see him. Course, I can't speak for the weekends, but I think it highly unlikely.'

'Let me get this straight. He had no contact at all with the outside world?'

'There'd be the occasional telephone call. Very occasional.'

'What a queer way to live.'

'It was the way he wanted to live. It was he who cut himself off, you know, Inspector. He couldn't bear to let his old friends see him. See what he'd become. We'd sometimes walk down into the village in the evening, and passers-by really would stop and stare at him. Sir Paul knew it. And, in spite of all his bluster, it hurt.'

'He couldn't have known, surely?'

'He *insisted* on knowing. He'd grill me after every encounter. Did they stare? Did they gawp? Did they blanch? What did they say? He had to know. He had to drink his poison to the very last drop.'

'Brrrr, a bit too creepy for me.'

'If that's how you feel, Inspector, think how he felt.'

'True. A sad, sad case.'

'So it was just you and he together in this lonely old cottage?'

'Uh huh. Well, actually, no, when I first moved down here, there was a housekeeper who'd come in every day. A Mrs Kilbride, a local woman. But about a week after I arrived, she started having problems with her husband. I mean, *he* started having problems, health problems. He had a bad flu, then some kind of pneumonia, and now, I can't be sure, but he may have come down with something very serious. Lung cancer, I believe. Anyway, we saw less and less of her as time went by and she eventually dropped out of our lives altogether.'

'Who did the cooking – the – the dusting, the housework?'

'I did.'

'You're quite the Renaissance man, Mr Ryder.'

'I've always lived alone. If I don't do it, no one else will. At home, I mean.'

'I see . . . Ah, Willie, there you are. I was just about to call you. I think Mr Ryder here has told me everything he knows.'

'Which wasn't much, I'm afraid.'

'Never expected it to be. So? Turn up anything of interest?'

'Could be, sir. Or could be nothing.'

'Well, what is it?'

'A diary.'

'*A diary!*'

'Where'd you find it?'

'In Sir Paul's bedroom. Tucked away in a drawer beneath a pile of old newspapers. It was locked, but I, eh, I managed to open it. Fact, I found quite a few of these notepads in there. This one looks like it's the most recent, though. And what's interesting is –'

'But that's impossible!'

'Just a moment, Mr Ryder. What were you saying was interesting, Sergeant?'

'But, Inspector, I tell you, there can't be a diary. Not Sir Paul's diary. The man was blind, he didn't have any eyes! How could he have kept a diary!'

'Sergeant?'

'It's his, all right. Got his name on the cover.'

'But he couldn't write! What do you suppose I was here for?'

'Well, that's it, you see, Mr Ryder. As you'd expect, it's all handwritten. And the writing's really terrible. It all slants to one side just like – Oh God, what do you call it?'

'What?'

'When writing slants. You know, like in a book?'

'Italics?'

'Italics. That's it, Inspector, that's the word. It's like it's all written in italics. Page after page of it.'

'Okay, Willie, but what was so interesting? What you were about to say?'

'Just that this one, this particular notepad, seems to start with the arrival of Mr Ryder here.'

'Really?'

'Yeah. Listen. "The blind is flapping at the window again. I don't care what anyone says, there really has to be a draught somewhere." Blah blah blah blah blah. Then he continues, "Ryder will be ringing the doorbell any minute now, or so I hope. He's late already. Slightly as yet, but late all the same. I can't abide" – can't quite make this next word out. Begins with a v or maybe it's a u.'

'Just go on.'

'"What was it someone said? That the trouble with – with – punctuality" – punctuality, right – and, yes, now I get it, the word in the sentence before was "unpunctuality". "I can't abide unpunctuality. What was it someone said? That the trouble with punctuality is that there's never anyone there to appreciate it. Well, I would have been here to appreciate it! Though, to be fair, if he has motored down from London, it's possible the weekend – the weekend – traffic has been heavy."'

'That it?'

'No, there's more. "So, Mr Ryder. There you are and here I am. We shall see what we shall see." "We shall see what we shall see." Funny language for a blind man to use.'

'Mmm. Though, in an odd way, you don't have to have known him to get the feel of the sort of man he must have been. Is there a lot more of the same?'

'Yup. He seems to have written in it fairly regularly. Here's something about you, Mr Ryder. "Somewhat colourless, at least so far, but that's all right and he'll – he'll – he'll –"'

'What's the problem, Sergeant?'

'Words stuck together. Oh, I get it. It's "probably thaw" – "he'll probably thaw". But it's written like it's a single word – "probablythaw". Here's another – "allinall" all bunched up together. Normal, I suppose. Poor fellow couldn't see what he was writing.'

'Okay. Read on.'

'"He'll probably thaw as we get to know each other. Inevitable if he's to live here, so – so – deference isn't a bad point of departure. Not too stupid, either, which is convenient. No, all in all, I think I've made a good and suitable choice. God knows, I might have done worse." Well, that's a bit of a mixed notice, Mr Ryder. But on the whole good, I suppose.'

'Any of the entries dated?'

'Doesn't look like it, sir. Wait a moment – no – no, it isn't. "I know now I've taught myself nothing, memorized nothing. All those years and nothing to show for them. I'm helpless, helpless – and, save for John, completely alone in the world. Sightless, eyeless, faceless and alone – and alone" – don't know what this is – "au" – "auf" – no, it looks like a "t". Could it be "autistic"?'

'All right, assume it's "autistic".'

'"Sightless, eyeless, faceless and alone, autistic, visually autistic, exiled from the – from the – humdrum – the humdrum – the humdrum – vibrancy of the world. Oh, has anyone ever, ever been in such desperate straits? What is that world to me now but a blank sheet of paper, a blank blank sheet of paper" – no, wait, I think it's – yeah – it's "a blank *black* sheet of paper – a blank black sheet of paper from which every trace of text is fading fast. What I would give – my right arm, my left arm, my legs, my nose, my fingers, my" – well, sir, what it says is – "my cock, everything! – for one more glimpse of that world!" Oh dear, oh dear. He *was* in a bad way.'

'All right, Willie. A little respect. It goes on, does it?'

'Yes, sir. Fills the book, nearly.'

'Good. Well, Mr Ryder, if you don't mind, I think we'll take this along with us.'

'I –'

'As I said, it might just give us an insight into the poor man's frame of mind at the end. Who knows?'

'And I'm very grateful you could give us so much of your time. Sergeant?'

'Please don't bother seeing us out. And thanks again. If we need you for anything, we know where to get in touch. Goodbye, Mr Ryder.'

'Goodbye.'